The Visionary

By Melody Hope

THE VISIONARY

First edition. November 2, 2024.

Copyright © 2024 Melody Hope.

ISBN: 979-8227559234

Written by Melody Hope.

Thanks

I want to give the biggest thanks to the artist who painted the cover art and a special thanks to David Ochab and Jessica Farrell for assisting me in editing. Thank you for believing in this story and believing in me! I couldn't fully bring this world to life without the support from all of you.

I'm so grateful for all my readers! Thank you for supporting me all these years! I appreciate you. Whether you've been here before my first story or my recent one! There's been so much growth and change in my writing, but I doubt that will stop anytime soon! So, I'll see you around!

All love,
Melody Hope

I used to ask what this world's purpose was. What was my purpose in it? It seems that humans were made to simply survive day by day while doing trivial activities to pass the time. Pass the time to what, though? Where are we going as a human race? Things in our world are only getting worse.

Looking back it was all clear, but only a few could see the signs. Imagine! What if everything you knew of your normal life was a lie? What if everything authors made up in books about creatures, gifts, and other life were all true? What if we, as humans, are the real mutants, but have been stripped down to our basics to give those with a craving for power to dominate?

It may sound far-fetched but hear me out. Watch the way dancers slide across the stage. Sometimes it seems as if they could fly. Yet, what if those who danced were meant to fly?

What if the troubled life we know is in an unnatural state and it's finally falling apart at the corners? How do we know this and more importantly, who are we? We're the people who are helping the earth grow back to its natural state to something better. But for me to have you understand we need to start at the beginning. Well, my beginning...

Chapter One

The surrounding walls tremble. Underneath the doors, in the safe bunker, they heard the crash of household items being displaced.

Riona's parents huddled around her, holding her tightly. Wincing slightly at every noise that came from above. From the rattles and thuds, Riona could only imagine what was happening. The longer it went on the more her parents squeezed her harder.

"They're not going to stop," Riona's father tells his wife. "They know we're here and they will demolish this house to find us. I don't think we can wait this out."

"What about Riona?"

"We've protected her all these years. They don't know she exists."

Riona looks between them hearing their words and studying their silent language. She sat there trying to figure out what they had in mind but all she could think to say was, "No!"

She felt her parent's hands on her, their faces looking at her tenderly.

"They won't give up until they have us. We will all be dead if we don't go," her father explains.

"There has to be another way!" Riona bargains. "We have to do something- anything! Maybe I can help you!"

Her mother leans in to kiss her daughter's worried face. "You'll be okay," she whispers in her ears. "It's okay."

Riona clenches her teeth with tears pouring from her eyes. "No, please. Let me help!"

Her father leans in, embracing his family. "You listen to me Riona, okay?"

Riona buried her head into her parents knowing she couldn't stop them. Clinging to them she never expected their worst fears to catch up to them. She didn't even know the whole truth, they never told her. They always told her they were protecting her until she was older. She was seventeen and abided by everything they structured for her. It was because of their jobs that they would never be a normal family. They couldn't risk her becoming a target, too.

Listening, she could tell they were going to tell her what to do next.

"We're going to give ourselves up. They don't know you're in here. As soon as we leave we have the house set to be locked. Don't leave this house until someone we trust comes and gets you. Okay? The people we know will have the right code to get you once they find out what has become of us."

"Ahhhh!" Riona screams. Something hit the house hard, shaking their balance.

"We haven't much time sweetheart, okay? We have to leave now," Mother says cupping her checks in her hands. "We love you."

Bringing the family to their feet Father kisses the top of both of their heads. "Everything will be fine."

Riona wished she could understand. Her body quivered as her parents pulled away from her, walking backwards until they reached the ladder.

"Be strong," they tell her. "You will always carry us with you."

Riona's face now wet with tears watches as her worst fear has come to life. Her agonizing voice prevailed through her cracked voice, "I love you!"

Her mother blew her a kiss before climbing onto the ladder with her father, leaving her all by herself. Riona hugs herself when she hears the safe door latch above. Shutting her eyes tightly she could still hear what sounded like weapons being used against the house. But not long after her parents left the sounds abruptly stop.

Lifting her chin upwards, she was surprised at the sudden silence. Looking around the bunker she saw all the food her parents had stashed away on their many shelves on the floor.

Stepping over them she made her way to the ladder and up to the house. Touching the knob she drew her hand away, wondering what that door would expose her to. She knew she had to do it, though.

With the door cracked open Riona saw the furniture was displaced or flipped over. Any pictures and fixtures that hug from the walls had all come down.

Maneuvering through the mess she made her way to the window. She had to know what was going on outside. Her parents had made the windows tinted so no one could see inside. So, if there was anything to be seen she would be made inconspicuous. Riona's parents had all sorts of gadgets from being undercover agents.

Looking outside she peers out as far as she can only to find there was no disturbance whatsoever. No people, no cars, no damage. Nothing at all. Riona knew better to ask about their jobs, but it didn't always add up. Her gut told her there was more to it. Plus, who could have such weapons to do this to their home and leave no trace of their destruction afterwards?

Everything was quiet. Too quiet. Looking at the neighbor's homes, no one seemed disturbed. It was as if no one saw that anything had happened. How was that possible?

Closing the curtain she turns back to face her reality. Her parents told her to be strong, so she had to be, but she was alone. Completely alone. Riona drops to the floor, hugging her knees, letting her cries of confusion, anger, and uncertainty tumble out of her.

Next thing she knew she woke in a haze. As the fog in her mind lifted she rushed back to the window. Everything had been the way it was before, except it was dark.

She sat wondering how long it would take for someone to come and get her. Until then, she took matters into her own hands. She couldn't sulk and feel sorry for herself. All she had was herself and she had to make the best of it. She had to take care of herself. Her parents would want that. The question was, what do to first?

A wave of dizziness came across her, but then realized what she must do. Pushing herself on she made her way back down to the bunker. Flipping on the light to illuminate the darkness, she searches for something appealing to eat. She never expected the years of hoarding goods would ever come into use. Apparently, her parents had thought of everything.

Of course, nothing sounded appealing, let alone to make a home-cooked meal. She saw a packet of combos lying at her feet and grabbed it.

Taking it back upstairs she eats them as she walks through the house. With her head already clearer she puts what was left of her home back together.

Riona flips the couch back upright, shifts the side tabled straighter, places the frames of her parents and herself into a pile, and cleans up any broken glass on the floor. It was something to do to keep herself busy until she knew what to do with herself next.

She turns her head toward the door. It would be so easy to pack up and go find answers, but her parents were smart. They knew the situation better so she had to obey and stay put. For now. She knew little of the world outside. Where would she go anyway?

Then an idea came into her mind. With her parents being "undercover agents" they had some pretty nifty gadgets. There may be a lot more to this house than she knew. Maybe the house itself held the answers to the questions she was searching for.

Circling in place she looks over the house with a new perspective. If anything were hidden where would it be? She positions herself in the front of the door. Deciding to start at the very beginning to search every inch of the house. She started feeling with her hands every tile on the floor to every brick on the walls.

Reaching the carpet she pats it roughly. Nearing the side wall, her hands stop. Not quite sure what it was she slid her fingernails into the side edges of the carpet to pull it up. On the hardwood, she saw a little bent-up contraption. Picking it up she concluded it was a weapon of some sort. Though she had never seen many weapons before.

Examining it, she pulled it apart, and up came a sharp edge. She rests the soft padding of her finger on the small of it, feeling it. She flinches slightly on the touch. "I wonder why that was there."

With an inner light of hope rising inside of her, she knew there was more to discover. Her deep search of the house continued with her trusty knife.

Days, weeks, and nearly a month went by since she found the knife. Nothing else. And what was worse, no one came to get her.

She uses a wooden board by the door and stabs her knife into it, slicing down a line. A line next to many other lines. Counting her days of being alone.

Every time she marked another day she would stand facing the door. Contemplating whether or not she would decide to leave or continue to live in her empty home. That's when she made up her mind on the 30th day when she was done searching the house from top to bottom, if she hadn't found anything she would leave.

In the kitchen, she tried to keep everything organized but the trash accumulating was overflowing. Thankfully her thorough search was done. All she had left was the rooms she didn't want to search. Her own room and her parent's room.

Standing in the doorway of her parent's room for the first time since everything went down, she couldn't help the hurt she felt from not knowing what happened to them. If they were still alive or not. Pulling on the knobs on her mom's drawers she began removing her clothes, laying most of them on the bed. When she came across one of her mom's old sweaters, Riona ran her hand over it, feeling it. She always liked that cardigan. It was the softest thing she had ever felt. She remembered telling her mother as much. Sniffing it she pulls it close to her briefly before putting it on.

Searching down the drawers she found more clothes, but pulling at the very bottom drawer it was lighter. "Pictures!"

She sat on the floor slowly going through each of them. A lot of them were pictures of her parents when they were younger. She saw them training together. Others were wedding pictures. They didn't seem to be too enthused in the pictures, but they must have been happy. The last stack of pictures were of them as a family. All of them together here in the house. Here is where Riona could tell they never looked happier, although it was weird to see herself as a baby. She had never seen one in real life.

Riona continues her search. High and low. Her father's drawers, their closest, there was nothing that revealed to her that they were agents. Wouldn't agents have more on them? Weapons, a safe, a badge at least? Riona gathers her thoughts. She never saw their badges. Perhaps if they got caught with them it would blow their cover?

Riona sighs. There was no evidence of who her parents were. It made her wonder if they were at all what they said. More so, if they were hiding more than she thought.

Becoming overly frustrated at trying to figure this out she took her knife and flung it across the room. It stuck in the side wall with a thud. Going to get it she pulls it out to throw it again. "Uhh!" Thud.

"Why did you do this to me!" she yells.

Yanking the knife out again to send it flying once more. Thang! "Huh?"

The knife hadn't made its usual thud. The sound difference brought Riona's mind back into focus. Readily examining it. The drywall felt the same on the outside. Knock knock. She uses her knuckles to examine the sound better. Knock knock.

Finding the differing sounds in only a small corner she raises her knife to cut around it. Prying the drywall off she wondered aloud to herself, "what is that?"

A book seemed to be wedged into the wall. It looked like it had been there for quite some time. Attempting to take hold of it to slip it out, it fell to the ground. It was an old brown leather journal book.

Collapsing to the floor she opens the book, starting at page one. It started with journals of her childhood. In her mother's handwriting. It explained some things.

"Today we watched little Riona playing on the floor. We can see how much potential she has. To be something amazing. To do something we won't be able to accomplish. She is the purest thing in life we've ever seen."

"We've decided not to send Riona to public school. Maybe if we separated ourselves from what we do we could have a chance at normal life. But we've come so far, there's no chance of that. The alliance needs us."

"Alliance?" Riona whispers confused.

Flipping through the pages she sees that they were filled with passages of her growing up. If that's all, why hide it? There had to be more to this journal if it was so protected. Back and forth through the pages she studies everything. It was all about her and how her parents cared and loved her.

"Wait a second." Riona realizes something. She knew her parents handwriting well. No one else may have noticed, but intertwined with her mother's penmanship some of the letters in her words looked like her father's.

Ripping out a blank page she starts at the beginning, writing every lone letter her father had written. Slowly those letters started coming together as words on her paper. How they knew she would figure this out was beside her, but if she was anything like her parents then perhaps they assumed she would pay attention to the details.

"I did it." She smiles down at the paper. She imagines in her mind that her parents were praising her, "Good girl. Keep going."

She read the words aloud, trying to make sense of it all. "Riona, if anything ever happens to us remember what we told you when you were little. It would always keep you safe."

Squinting her nose she repeats, "it will always keep me safe?" Her eyes widen remembering something when she was smaller. Her parents had come home with a present. A white teddy bear...

"Thank you! I love it!" Riona hugged the teddy bear tightly against her chest.

Father knelt on his knees. "I want you to remember something. If anything were to ever happen to mommy and daddy, Teddy will always keep you safe...."

Riona rushes to her bedroom. It was one of the last toys she had but she always cherished it. Could that really be the answer to all this?

"It would always keep me safe."

Picking the little ragged teddy bear in her hands she looks around it, under its bow tie, around his eyes. Well, they could have been cameras! Pulling back the fur on its back she examined the threading. The thread was a little thicker than the rest of the threading.

"Sorry little guy," she says flipping up her knife upwards. Being careful she cuts up the seam.

She picked at the bunched-up stuffing and her hand hit something. Grabbing a hold of it she lifts it out. It was a folded piece of paper. Sitting on the bed, Teddy behind her, she carefully opens the paper trying to figure out what it would tell her.

Our dear Riona. If you find this letter it may have meant something has happened. Without going into great detail you must know that everything

you see around you in this world is a lie. We're not undercover agents in any government. We're a part of an alliance in hopes of bringing about something good. We did everything the way we did in your upbringing to keep you safe. We wanted to give you some normality to your childhood. When you turned the age of 18 we were going to explain everything to you. We wanted to let you choose if you wanted to follow in our footsteps or make another life for yourself. Right now, if you are reading this you have nowhere to go and no one to trust. That is why we are giving you the address of the alliance. Memorize it and burn this letter. If the people that we know are still at the agency they will know who you are. They will fill you in on everything. Take care little Riona. You are stronger than you know. We love you. Mom and Dad.

Riona covers her mouth taking in every word, dissecting it. Her whole life was a lie. She understood that it was for her protection but her parents should have told her long before now. Determined not to live with being mad at them she took action instead.

Scurrying across the room she grabs her backpack in the back of the closet. A backpack she always used for play of course, since she had never been outside the house before. It made a lot more sense now why she had it.

She stuffs it with needed clothing and what she thinks may be essential. Lastly, she stuffs her teddy bear into it along with an old family picture that sits on her desk. This was her journey now. Her life and choices were in her hands.

Buttoning her mother's cardigan in the front she swings her backpack onto her shoulders. Pocket knife in hand she made her way to the door. Until now she never realized how intimating a door could be. A whole new world lay in front of her. And a world of lies? What did that mean?

But oh! The letter she held so tightly in her hand. She had already forgotten to burn it. Walking to the kitchen she read over the note one last time. Memorizing the address.

Next to the stove was a drawer and in it she found matches. Taking one she lit it and slowly tilted the paper until was grasped by the flame. Sitting it down on top of the stove she left it to burn. Her time had come to leave and leave she did.

Chapter Two

Standing on the porch she looks both ways of the street. She had two options. Deciding to play it safe she starts in the direction she had seen her parents leaving before.

Walking the side of the road an occasional car passed. Even a few kids with their bikes went by. Riona would watch them go. People were out doing their daily things. How were these things, that looked so innocent be deceitful? Despite how things looked she was very careful of what was around her. Hopefully she would know more soon.

When she came to a split in the road she looks left then right. Another decision had to be made. Thinking hard she tries to remember all those times she watched her parents leave. She could just make out this turn from the house. Which way had she seen them go?

"Miss. You lost?"

Riona jumps. Turning, she saw an older man cleaning his front yard. She hadn't noticed him watching her. "Ah. No! Thank you."

The older man nods and bent back to what he was doing. He didn't seem like a bad person. Maybe he could help. But, would that be wise? She looked back at the man. There was nothing about him that said he was untrustworthy. She had to get to her destination somehow.

"Sir?"

The man looks up. "Yes, miss?"

"Have you seen a black van come up and down this road a lot?"

"A black van." He stops to think. "Yes, I think I have."

"Do you remember which way it turns?"

"Well. My memory is not what it used to be, but I want to say it turns to the right."

"Ah! Yes! Thank you." Riona tries to act as if she had known all along so he wouldn't get suspicious. If, of course, there was anything to be suspicious about.

"No problem, miss!" He waves her off.

The old man may have been right, she thought. After some time she came up on a bunch of older buildings. Perhaps one of those buildings would be the address she needed. Keeping a look out she tries to catch every address to see if the numbers would add up. The numbers didn't seem to be too far off. Could the alliance really have been so close to home?

She walks until dusk broke. That's when she comes across a huge warehouse. Scanning the huge building she realized she couldn't find the door. Walking on the next street over she found what could be the front.

Searching for an address she found an old mailbox laying in the grass. She circles it seeing some of the warn off numbers. This was it! This was place! It looked dark and abandoned, but this was it. It's was worth a shot at least. Wait- she noticed. The door had no handle. How odd.

Little did she know while she stood outside what was happening inside. High above her were tinted windows and behind those windows a young man was watching her.

"Astra!" He calls down to the blond haired woman below.

"What's up Riv!" She looks up to him from the ground floor.

"We've got a girl outside the door."

Astra crinkles her face. Everyone was in for the night. Had they forgotten someone? "Do you recognize her?"

Riv leans in closer to the window. "Brown hair. Bright blue eyes."

Astra places a hand on her hip. "You want me to give you two a moment?"

Riv turns his head to look down at her expressionless.

Astra laughs at her own tease, "I got it!" Astra goes to the door and opens it a crack to see the girl in front of her jump backwards. "Hey kid, I didn't mean to scare ya. What'cha doing?"

"Ah- well- I."

The woman in front of her raises her eyebrows waiting for her to form a comprehensible sentence.

"I'm Riona," she rushes.

Astra turns away, thinking a moment. "Something happened to them, didn't it?"

"If you're talking about my parents, yeah. I think something bad happened. Otherwise, I don't think I would have found the clues they left for me to find this place. The letter said you would know who I was."

"Yeah kid, I know who you are." Her face became downcast before opening the door wider, motioning her to come inside.

On doing so she shouts, "she's good Riv."

Though Riona didn't know what that meant she looks around the empty building before her chin turns upwards. She could just make out a figure sitting in the darkness. The white of his eyes were enough to give him away. He was watching them. No, that wasn't right. Her stomach twinged. He was watching her.

Turning her attention back down she kept up with the woman she was following.

"We knew this day could come but we hoped it wouldn't."

Riona found herself being lead around the corner to an open and empty bedroom.

"This will be where you'll stay for the time being. Make yourself at home. Feel free to wander about the warehouse. As long as you don't disturb anyone at this hour I really don't care what you do. Oh, my name is Astra. If you need anything the intercom is on the wall."

"Astra," Riona calls out. "I know very little of what happened. Can you fill me in?"

"Tomorrow." Astra nods coolly before walking out.

"Oh, okay."

Riona had found her way and yet she still felt so alone. Though, it was her first away from home. And being in such a unfamiliar place she knew she wouldn't be getting much sleep. Climbing up on to the bed she took a hold of her teddy and held him as close as she could.

Chapter Three

"Where are we?" Riona asks as she follows Astra into a darkened room. The room was filled with theater seats and up front a stage was lit.

"Sit," Astra tells her after sliding into one of the rows.

On doing so Riona watches Astra place her feet over the next row of chairs. "Astra." Riona looks around the room. "Why is there a theater in this old warehouse? This is a theater, right?"

"As it has been created, yes."

"Really!" Riona exclaimed in excitement.

"But not for what you think. I figured this would be the best place to catch up. This room is essentially one of many rooms we have here. All for teaching purposes."

"To teach what?" Riona looks up curiously.

"Riona, I'm not gonna lie. I don't know how to do- this. So, I'm just gonna start at the beginning and hopefully you'll be able to fill the rest in."

"O-okay."

"When your parents were about your age they joined the alliance here. It was ran by a man named Shar. This alliance has been passed down generation after generation for one sole purpose. Your parents probably didn't tell you everything, but the entire world as we know it is a lie. The human race is essentially in a cage. The rest of Earth, as it should be, is completely shut off from us. This is all due to a war that took place a very long time ago. Between those who thought order should be kept and those who wanted to let things progress naturally, as it had been. Those people, who demanded such order, became what we call Rouges. They gathered against us with sophisticated weapons of technology and put us in this cage. This life as we know it is in an unnatural state. Now, your parent's under cover mission was to become government officials to see how many of these Rouges were working on the inside of things. It was our way of staying one step a head of them. That way we can find the boundaries of these caged walls and figure out a way to take it down. Which, of course, may lead to another war. But, over the decades we have been recruiting people to aid us in this fight."

Riona opens her mouth for only air to escape. She didn't know what to expect from this place. But if everything Astra said was true, it was hard to fathom. "I-I don't know what to say."

"So, how much did you know?" Astra asks her.

"Apparently nothing. I knew about the undercover agents, but I knew nothing."

"They kept things pretty sheltered for ya, eh?"

"That would be an understatement."

Riona looks to the stage where she saw a man and woman in their dance attire. Dancing, spinning, and jumping all over the place. As individuals they were good but together, "oh they're awful!"

Astra laughs at her. "They're not training to dance."

"What?"

"When this cage, or barrier, was put up around us it robbed us of who were. Individually, the identity of our species, and what came with that identity. Our gifts."

"Wait." Riona shifts in her seat excitedly. "Are you saying we all have superpowers?"

Astra gives her look. "In a sense. Those dancers up there are some of our newer recruits.

Since they previously had a life in dancing we thought it was possible they came from the Farillia species."

"Far- what?"

"The closet to your understanding what be fairies."

"They're fairies? Wait! Wait. My parents always read me bed time stories. Stories of fairy tales and all things no one would really believe. Are you saying those make believe stories are true?" Riona clutches the arm of her chair, eating up every word Astra told her.

"In a sense, yes."

"If some held that understanding of what is real then why make them into children's books?"

"They were created by those who could see past this fake world into what was truly real. But, they may not have fully understood or saw the full scope of things."

"Astra, to find out what my gifts are I need to know who I am, right?"

Astra looks at her. "That is something you must figure out for yourself."

"That's not fair!"

"I can't awaken something that you're not ready for. You may have a gift or maybe you don't. You need to figure that out yourself."

Riona furrows her brows. "That's why you have all these training rooms?"

"I knew you were smart." Astra smiles at her.

"You're not gonna put me in a pink tutu and see if I can fly are you?"

"If it helps! Naaa," she waves her joke off. "Today you're just getting settled. Come. I'll show you around."

Not far from them sounds of gasping and awes came from the stage. Capturing Astra and Riona's attention. Riona raises her head to see one of the dancers floating in mid air from his leap while the rest of the class gathered around to watch them in awe.

"Ahh!" He tries to balance himself before floating down rather quickly. He landed on his feet in a crouched position.

"He's okay," Astra assures her. Clearly seeing her flinch. "They're advanced students. Plus Farillias have quite the health and stamina to prevent them from getting hurt. Most of the time." Astra pushes Riona out of the aisle. Letting her follow behind once again.

It wasn't too far down the corridor she turns and walks them under an open arch. At far end of the wall were stack of books, containers, bandages, and doctor equipment. In the middle were a few beds.

A woman stood with her back toward them, tinkering with something in her hands.

"Kou, this is Riona. Riona this Kou. She's our nurse, Doctor, surgeon, ect."

Kou turned around to shake Riona's hand. "It's a pleasure to meet you Riona."

Riona smiles up at her brightly. "The pleasure is mine! I've never meet a Doctor before."

"I'm not a typical Doctor. I do have learned knowledge of course, but my gift is to heal. A lot of my knowledge is intuition."

"That's amazing! I'm still figuring out where I fit in with all of this. I wouldn't be disappointed if I had your gifts, though."

"Kou, Riona has just gotten here. Could you give her a quick check up? Make sure she healthy for training tomorrow?"

Kou nods. "Of course." Kou motions for Riona to sit on one of the beds. On doing so Kou simply looks over her face and head before skimming down her body visually.

Riona watches her every move trying to figure out what she was doing. "How does everything look?" she asks curiously.

"Everything looks very well! You seem to have a lower immunity for someone your age, but nothing that can't be strengthened."

"Kou," Astra chips in, "can you tell if she's awakened her gift yet?"

Riona stares intensely between Astra and Kou. Could they really tell her that?

Kou moves her hands around the sides of her head feeling. "I see it." Kou acknowledges. "It's neither completely doormat nor fully awakened. I cannot tell you what stage she is in, but it is there. Which, is promising that she could any time. It's very rare for one to never access any part of their gift at all. With the proper training I have no doubt Riona may very soon be introduced to it."

Astra nods her thanks, "thank you, Kou."

Jumping off the table Riona surprises Kou with a hug. Before Kou could say anything more she was left watching Riona leave with Astra.

Entering into the main area of the floor there was an area set a side for physical activities. "This is the combat training ring." Astra points. "Some do have physical gifts, but most have learned. This is a training course all of us must take. We have yet to learn the kind of war we'll be fighting. So, we're doing our best to prepared."

Riona observes the two opponents going after each other, deflecting one another blows equally. Riona could tell they were well trained with how smoothly they seemed to bounce back and react. The man and woman in the ring were very fit. It made Riona feel conscious of her petite body frame. She wasn't very tall either. Was she really expected to learn combat? She understood the preparation, but it seemed to require so much physical effort. That is one thing she hadn't done growing up inside the house.

"Our trainer is Riv. He's the best we have. He isn't gifted in physical combat but he is a natural at it."

Riona looks over to get a better view of Riv. He was crossed armed and very focused on the training session in front of him. He was analyzing his students. Riona thought he kind of looked like the same man she saw yesterday when she arrived.

Astra walks on and Riona speeds up her pace to catch her. On doing so Astra pushes a button on the wall to open a door that beeped.

"Get in."

"What is this?" Riona steps cautiously in.

"It's called an elevator."

The doors beeped again and began to close.

Between the gap of door in motion Riona continued to watch the training in the combat ring. She found it intriguing. In that same moment Riv turns his glance to them in the elevator. Or so Riona thought. As the door shut the elevator shook, involuntarily making her shoulders tighten slightly at the unexpected motion.

"I see we have a lot of work to do."

Riona stares at the silver doors. Waiting for them to open again. She wouldn't be scared this time. She wouldn't!

Beep. The doors slide open. Riona didn't flinch.

Following Astra off the elevator she tells her what this level was for. "A lot of the Brainies are up here. Or, that's what we call them. Don't ask me to pronounce the long official title. They're in tune with all things technological. They've been working hard to learn the Rouges technology and see if we can't break the barrier they've put up around us. I do mean literally. Wall, field, barrier. Whatever you want to call it. I know we can do it, but this cage is also hindering our gifts full potential."

They pass widows of a dark room. Many young men and women sat facing their computers. Without using a keyboard or mouse they were controlling the screens by their minds alone.

"How close are you to shutting it down?"

"We hope close. Once the threat is sensed the Rouges redo everything. Like resetting a password and making it harder. We're currently testing out a new virus that we hope won't be noticed until too late. If the tests and simulations are promising we'll be tying it out at our next ready attempt to win our earth back."

"Is there anyone on the outside who could help us?"

"Rouge spies? Not a chance. Well, I guess you never know but I haven't heard of anything."

"I meant more of us on the other side. Fighting from both sides of this wall."

"Oh. Yes. It's likely. Communicating with them would hold a tremendous risk, though. And if there is, they're just as much as a prisoner on this earth as we are caged here."

"Hmm."

"Why? Do you have any bright ideas Riona?"

"Hmm?" Riona was lost in thought. Processing all Astra told her. Wondering if and how she could contribute to this mission of theirs.

"You seem to be deep thinker. Perhaps the psychic room will be right up your ally. Up ahead." Astra points.

Through the wide open windows Riona observes groups doing a different kind of training. In one corner there were a few taking up soft round balls and raising them into the air. Suspending them in air above their hands. Yet, in another group a trainer held out flash cards for them to guess what was on the other side.

"Many who develop their gift is a feat alone. Though all our gifts come from the same part in the brain they all have distinct feature. Some are more common while others are more rare. Some have one and some have a few. We have those who can see or hear thoughts, some know the feelings of others, and some can see something happen before its happened. Over there, in that group, we have those who can manipulate physical objects."

"The force is real." Riona's child like eyes look up at Astra.

"Riona, what on earth do you mean? Sometimes I follow you and other times I worry."

Riona lifts her hands moving her fingers. "Jedi tricks."

Astra turns away from Riona to look back at the class. "They left me to raise a child."

"What?" Riona's lowers her voice into to a whisper. "I guess she hasn't seen Star Wars."

"Of course," Astra makes her way back up the hall, "there are many kinds of gifts we don't have here. Until you discover who you are I want you to take every class. See if anything rings true to you."

As they step back into the elevator Riona was moving with excitement over these possibilities. "Will you be my trainer?"

"We'll see," Astra tells her as she watches the elevators doors close on them. "As of right now I'm giving you the rest of the day to think about everything you've seen and learned today. I can imagine you have a lot to think about."

"Oh," Riona looks down at her feet. I guess she could understand that. It probably should be overwhelming for her. She did just lose everything, but she'd rather keep herself busy here. It would be what her parents would have wanted too. And if she could contribute and help them somehow. Maybe she could help the alliance find out what happened to them. Maybe they could still find them.

"Astra, what will happen to my parents? Can we not- you know. Go get them?"

Astra turns to face her. "Riona, if they're still alive they've most likely been taking to one of their holdings outside our boundaries. There's nothing we can do for them right now but believe they're strong enough to take care of themselves."

Pressing her lips together she nods her head. It made sense. It made her feel better knowing she had hope of seeing them again. That they weren't gone. Not yet.

Once the elevator stops Astra went her own way and Riona made her way back to her room. She should be questioning everything. Cautious that Astra was in fact telling her the truth. But her parents trusted these people, this alliance.

Plopping onto her bed a deep feeling within in told her she was right where she should be. That gave her mind peace. More so than when she first arrived.

Her first night here she couldn't help but toss and turn all night, clutching on to her bear. So, with her extra time to spare she climbs under her blankets to rest. Thinking over the many possibilities she drifts off to sleep in between thoughts.

When her eyes flicker open she sees the time on her clock near her bed, showing her how late in the night it was. She sat up with a start realizing what she had done. She must have been more tired then she realized. Flaring the blankets off, she jumps out of bed.

Cracking her door open and peeking out she sees the lights were off. As her graze drifted down she notices at her feet was a covered tin. Picking it up she took it inside. On lifting the cover she saw someone had graciously left her dinner.

She wondered who here was nice enough to have done so. For some reason she couldn't figure out if that would be Atra's thing to do. Going out of her way like that. Perhaps Astra had simply ordered someone to collect something for her. I guess it doesn't really matter, she tells herself.

Gouging down the meal of bread, meat, and veggies by her own hands she was then ready to explore the place a little more. Perhaps she could get into the computer room to play games or watch TV? If that was even a thing around here. Either way she still had the urge to explore the place and take her time without anyone watching over her.

Next to her bed, on her side stand, sat her pocket knife. She picks it up, putting it in her cardigan, before slipping out of her room.

Making her way to the combat ring she reaches out to touch it. Her eyes hadn't quite adjusted to the darkness yet, but something caught her eye on the wall nearby. Targets. Some were for bow and arrows as they sat up against the concrete wall. It was the other target that she was fascinated by, though. She recognized those marks.

With a hand in her pocket she wraps her fingers around her knife. Maybe she didn't know how to throw properly but it was a start. It was something she could tell Astra she could do! Sort of.

Flipping the knife up the small sound echoes in the emptiness of the warehouse. Gauging the distance she readies her stance. Being more aware of her posture than before. There had to be some order to this, right? Drawing her hands back she flings the knife at the target. Dung! The butt of the knife hit the target before falling.

Riona recomposes her stance, attempting to throw again. She was overthinking it, she knew it. She shifts back and forth on her feet and gave it another go. This time puncturing it! She shrills quietly.

Looking around she spots at the far end wall, near the elevator, looked like a star case. But the darkness concealed around it was far too intimidating to try it. Riona backs away slowly almost being scared of the unknown that lingered behind the darkness that she bumped into something hard. Turing around swiftly her hands clutches it. A ladder!

Her eyes follow the ladder up and notices it was some kind of high walk way up there. That didn't seem as intimating. The walkway was in line to the windows where the full moon was shining in, illuminating on the metal bars. A full moon would be a nice to see!

Climbing up the ladder she pulls herself cautiously onto the edge. She couldn't recall ever being this high before. Or ever. She took her time standing up. Holding on to the railing she slowly walks her way to other side where she saw a large window. Perfect for looking out and reflecting!

Walking her way over she hadn't realized until she reached the window that someone else was already there. "I didn't realize anyone was up here." Oh! She knew who he was. "I'm Riona. I heard them call you Riv?"

His shoulder length hair moves wispily as he turns to look at her, squinting, wondering who she was. "River."

"River!" she repeats his full name. Hearing the others address him differently she wasn't sure what to call him herself. "What do you prefer?"

With unwavering eyes and head tilted he took a moment before responding. "You can call me whatever you wish."

"I see." Riona lowers her head thinking before meeting his stare. "I do like the name River. I've never known anyone with that name before. Or, any name, I suppose."

"Do you always speak your mind? People don't do that, you know."

"Oh." She hadn't realized and she turns her head away. "Perhaps I do. I- uh. I haven't been around people much."

"Hmm. My people believe names tell you a lot about a person. Naming is taken very seriously."

Perking back up that River was adding to their conversation she asks him, "what does the name River mean for you?"

"I think the fact I was adopted changes things a little. A chief found me near the river. He took me as his own. I don't know where I came from, who my parents are, or what my tribe is. That doesn't matter now." River caught her nodding, taking all that he said in. He squints at her again. Why did she take an interest in him for? "What does Riona mean in your family?"

"Oh!" Blinking back to reality she forms her words to respond. "I was told it meant being pure. I think. I don't know what that meant to them. They always told me I'd end up doing great things because I would always have them with me." She turns her head away. "They were taken from me, so I'm not sure how I'm supposed to do that."

River strokes his smooth face contemplating. "Perhaps it does mean pure. I could see that in you. But from my knowledge of names it also means queen."

"Queen? I'm not sure if I'd measure up to being any sort of queen, but the thought is nice. Maybe it means I'll be something more than who I am today." Riona smiles trying to hide her sadness. "That's the hope anyways."

She still had many more people to meet in this new home of hers, but she was glad she meet River. Though, she had to admit the way he held himself was quite a mystery. If her gut told her anything it was that he was a good person, though. Despite his cold appearance.

Her mind kept replaying what he said. Him seeing that she was pure. How could he know that? They only just met. She couldn't shake the thought that meant something important in regard to who he was.

He already knew she spoke her mind, would it hurt to ask? "Is that part of your gift? To see things in people?" Though his expression seemed unchanged there was slightest shift in his face. Was he surprised at the question?

"Something like that."

"Can I ask you what your role here is with having that gift?"

River looks at the floors below. Unknown to Riona he was laughing to himself. He was the one to see rather than to be seen. Yet, she seemed to see exactly what he hid. Who was Riona? What was it that Astra saw in her? More importantly, what was her people? "I have the gift to see beyond the surface of things. I may feel a shift the in atmosphere. Those feelings form into thoughts to predict what may happen. It helps give us a heads up if there's anything we need to be prepared for."

"You're the alarm system." Riona was very intrigued, but at the same time she kept thinking about her parents. Could it be possible that she never really knew them? Who were her people? Riona began to feel she no longer knew who she was anymore either.

"What?" River stares at her.

"I don't know who I am or where I fit in with all of this. I know I want to help and make a difference but I don't know how. Astra won't tell me anything. She told me I had everything here at my disposal, but that I have to figure it out for myself. How do I know where to start?"

Riona could feel him watching her as she hung her head. She wondered if he was probing her with his gifts of knowing. It was nice to know if anyone could understand how she felt maybe it would be him.

Perhaps she needed to go back to her room and call it a night. Things may be more clearer in the morning. Plus, she ran out of things to say to River. He most likely wouldn't keep he convention going for the sake of small talk. "I think I'll head in for the night. It was nice to have met you River."

River nods her way before continuing his look out.

Chapter Four

Shifting in bed Riona groans. Her sleep really needed straightened out. Glancing over her shoulder at the clock it read: 6:00 am. Breakfast wasn't until 8:00. But maybe there was least someone else up.

Her bare feet slips out of the sheets and tiptoes across the cold floor. Cracking the door open she saw an outfit hanging on the other side. Bringing it in she remembered seeing a student wearing something similar. This must be her training outfit.

She replaced her casual clothes with a body fitting black tank and training pants. Even a black pair of shoes came with the attire. What was the meaning of black? Putting her foot in the shoe she drew it back just as fast. She felt something. Picking up the shoe she shakes it upside down. Falling to her lap were hair ties. "Well then," she smiles, "apparently it's a pony tail day."

A body mirror was tucked in the corner of her corridors. She moves it out and props it against the wall to look at her ensemble. It was defiantly a new look for her. She lay her hands over her flattened stomach before examining her tiny arms. There wasn't much muscle on her. Examining herself from the back side she sighs. There was still hope, right?

Gathering her hair to a pony tail she ties it off. She was as ready as she could be to start her first day of training. Hopefully her training would give her a glimpse into who she was in this world.

But she couldn't help but feel as if she was forgetting something. Oh! Her knife! It was the one thing she had from home. It was her source of security. Not that she didn't feel safe here but it was nice to know she had it with her.

With a jump in her step she opens the door, leaving her room. Turning the corner- "oof!" Riona ran right into River. He was leaning up against the side wall. Arms and leg crossed as if he'd been waiting for her.

Taking a hurried step back she realizes he didn't even flinch, let alone move.

"Good morning," Riona speaks hastily.

"I heard the door open a little bit ago. I figured you'd be out soon."

"Oh!" Riona shifts on her heels. Now at a loss for words.

"C'mon." Pushing himself off the wall River leads them out to the main floor.

She wasn't surprised that he started training before breakfast. Following him she found themselves standing in front the targets.

"You have your knife?" River asks, facing her.

She was about to question how he knew that when she remembered herself practicing last night. Instead of asking any questions she pulls the knife from her pocket, showing it to him.

"You have the basics down. Which is good." He took her knife. Demonstrating a stance. "Try this." With that stance and hand drawn back he let the knife fly. Hitting the target in the middle. "Got it?"

Riona nods her head trying to remember everything.

Once River retrieved the knife he hands it off to her. "You try."

She switches places with him and did her best to mimic his position. Trying to feel comfortable in it she shifts in her stance. Leary in her readiness.

Without warning River reaches out to stop her. Aligning his body posture with hers he puts his foot between her feet. Kicking one foot out. She didn't expect the movement and quickly tries to recover her balance, but maybe she shouldn't have. She wasn't sure. Soon after she felt a hand on her rib cage and one on her back. Lifting her back up to the proper posture.

Now she was in the right stance she could throw, right? She breaths in anticipation, but wait. He wasn't done yet. He reached out to take hold of her hand, arranging her fingers to hold her knife correctly. Was this how he trained his students?

She was still aware of his foot against hers, keeping her aligned. That made sense. Proper posture was a big deal in throwing correctly. But knowing how easy he was able to read her made her feel uneasy for some reason. She didn't know the full scope of his gifts, but the way he would look at her, it seemed as if he could see right through her. Like he could read her thoughts or feelings. It made her nervous and hyper aware the closer he was to her. As if he would hear or feel her more clearly.

Without thinking she said in her mind, "can you hear what I'm thinking?" She looks up, studying his determined face. Trying to figure him out.

River stops, turning his head to look at her.

Riona took in a tense breath and only hoped he wouldn't notice. Was that a coincidence that he looked at her or did he hear her? Averting her eyes she feels him pull away.

"Now throw," he directs her.

Throw she did. It flew through the air so fast and it hit the middle circle! She jumps in amazement. She hit it! She turns to River in her excitement, checking to see if he saw it.

A corer of his lips lifted sightly before pointing with his chin. "Now go get it and do it again." Happily she did just that. Practicing until she heard the breakfast bell ring.

It was then when they parted their ways, but not before River gave her a simple smile before heading off. Riona smiled back. She was grateful for the one on one training. She would take what she could get and make the best of it.

In the dining room, people gathered. The day now felt truly alive. She went through the breakfast line, mindlessly grabbing whatever looked good, before finding a place to sit. Not knowing everyone yet she wasn't sure where to go. Maybe she could go back to her room? Then, not too far away, she saw a more vacant table where Kou was sitting at the end.

"Hi." Riona smiles. "Can I join you?"

Kou looks up and smiles back. "Absolutely. How are thing going so far?"

Sitting down she tries to explain, "ahh. Well, things are still very new. Different than the life I used to know. Today will be my first day of training, but I'm excited!" On looking up Riona sees Astra on the other side of the room. "I think Astra is working out my schedule now." Astra was trying to show the paper that she held in hand with, oh, River! Was he to be one of her trainers? Assuming that the paper was in fact about her training schedule.

Kou caught her drift but took a different meaning to it. "That's Riv she talking to. He is one of the trainers. For your sake I hope you don't get him."

Riona focuses back on Kou. "What? Why?"

"He's a great trainer, but he's unpredictable. Aloof. I hear some complain he's too hard as a trainer. Don't get me wrong he's good but many question this methods."

Riona lifts her eyes to watch them again. Seeing River's emotions come to the surface. That was something she hadn't seen. Not like that. He began pointing at Astra in anger. Saying something she couldn't make out. He clearly wasn't happy. Was it about her?

Kou, now looking back over her shoulder, watches with Riona. They see him brush his way past Astra while she was still talking, leaving her looking agitated as well.

Riona watched River coming their way. She tries whispering his name as he came near. "Riv-er." But he doesn't stop, not even a glance.

"I told you." Kou make her point. "Unpredictable."

"Maybe you're right," Riona forces a smile. But the way he was when she was with him told her something different. Though she didn't know what, something was off.

Riona's thoughts were still whirling about that when she hears Astra's voice from behind she jumped. Astra had taken a seat next to her. Putting the paper down for Riona to see. So the fight was about her!

Riona scans the paper up and down, seeing what it was. It was her daily agenda. At the end of the day she saw that Riv was her last trainer. Was being her trainer what this was all about? River had already started helping her this morning! Things didn't make sense.

"Can you follow all this?"Astra broke her thoughts.

"Yeah, I think I can."

"Great!" Astra pats her shoulder before getting up to leave.

Propping her head up with both her hands Riona looks over the paper again seeing where she was at first. Doctor Kou Kawwa. Patient handling. "Looks I'm with you first." Riona glances up at Kou.

"Well then! Let's get started! I already have a patient for you."

In her office Riona waits near one of the tables as Kou went back to get their patient. Riona giggles as she sees the tiny bird. "Where did you find her?"

Kou sets the cage down on the bed. "Riv found her early this morning. We think she got hit by a car."

Riv huh? "What's wrong with her?"

Kou smiles, "to see if you have the gift of healing I'm not going to tell you that. Come here. Look her over. Let me know what you think." Kou's gently lifts the little bird out of the cage. The little bird sits on the bed. No eagerness to fly.

Riona examines the bird, looking to see if there was anything to see from a physical point of view. She saw nothing. Reaching out gently she strokes it's head gently with a finger.

"Good." Kou's praises. "You're in tune to her emotional state. Now, can you tell me what's hurting?"

Riona felt around the bird, down her head, her back, her wings. She then realizes if the bird was sitting with no eagerness to fly then maybe her wings were hurt or maybe her legs. "I think we need to take a look at her legs."

Kou picks the little bird up.

"Kou, I think one her legs are broken."

"How did you conclude that?"

"Well, seeing how she is holding herself and acting it's just a feeling."

"Good. Do you think you have the power to heal her?"

Riona's eyes waver. She felt for the little bird, she really did. She could somehow sense the pain, but to heal it? She wasn't sure. "How would I attempt to if I could?"

"Start with hovering your hands over the affected area while sensing the pain. Let it guide you. It'll feel like you're offering a little of your life to her. If you have the gift you'll know what to do."

Riona lifts her hands, letting go them around the birds legs, trying to sense the hurt. "I think I found the area!"

With Kou directing her on what to do next Riona closes her eyes. Now trying to give a part of herself and share it with the bird. Waiting for a feeling of passing. Taking another breath Riona tries again. "I don't think can," Riona says distraught. "I really wish I could help her."

Kou assures her. "That's alright. I don't think you have the gift of healing but you have such a giving heart. You could sense the pain. That's a good start in the right direction! Follow that instinct! Here," Kou places Riona's hand on top of hers, "I can put the healing power through you. It's not something I would normally do, but for you to understand what it would have been like I'll show you."

With their hands together Kou's healing gift flows through Riona to the bird. It was a kind of movement. As if something was leaving her own body. A feeling of giving.

The bird perks up, stretching legs cautiously before standing on it. Riona couldn't help but gasp in amazement.

"She's ready to fly." Kou puts the bird into Riona's hands.

"Thank you so much!" Riona beams.

Before heading to her next class she would take the bird outside. Pushing the door open she threw the bird up from her hold, letting it fly. She smiles in wonder as she watches the bird flapping and chirping away. "You're welcome."

On closing the door Riona stops to gaze upward. She had a hunch River may have been up there. She was right. Sitting at his usual spot looking out the window. Contemplating who knows what. She didn't disturb him and heads off to her next lesson.

Her next lesson was upstairs and instead of using the elevator she takes the stairs. She had to gain the muscle eventually, right? Every little bit would help! She ran up the stairs easily until reaching the next floor.

The first door on the right brought her the computer room. At the same moment of her arrival a young man opens the door to greet her.

"Hi Riona! I'm Leo. I'll be your trainer." He brought her into the darkened room. The only source of light came from the computer screens.

"Know anything about computes?" Leo asks her.

"Ahh- basics."

Leo smiles. "I can show you some of things were working on that you might be wondering about. So, if you have any questions hit me up anytime! Right now we'll see what skills you may have for this."

Riona presses her lips together, trying to hid her amusement. "In all honesty, I think I would laugh if this ended up being my gift."

"Let's find out!" Leo claps his hands together. "That screen on the wall in front of you. It's off. I want you to try to turn it on. Imagine, in your mind, that the screen is brightening. If you think of what you want it to do and it will."

"It'll just do it. That's what everyone is saying. It'll just happen. I've had nothing just happen yet. Expect for sensing a bird's pain."

Leo tells her to focus as she stares at the black screen. Long enough for her vision became blurry. She tries to blink the fog away but there was no use. She shakes her head at Leo.

"That's okay. You don't seem to have this gift. Even so, prior to Astra's direction, I'll show you a little more of what's been going on here."

"Like what?"

With his mind Leo turns on the screen. Riona watches the screen flip though files and images alike. All Leo had to do was think. He controlled it with such ease. When he stops he zooms in on a picture that looked like a wall. No, not a wall. A kind of barrier. It must have been what Astra was telling her about!

"It looks like some kind of field. It's all clear but something's there." Riona speaks her thoughts on the visual. "Like the kind of protection field from The Phantom Menace."

"Ah! You know your movies and tech!"

"Have you seen Star Wars?"

"Seen it! Everyone's seen it!"

"I made a Star Wars reference with Astra and you should have seen her face!"

Leo hands went to his knees, laughing. "I would have loved to see that!"

Getting back on track Leo explains more about the barrier. "This picture of the barrier is the closest from where we are located. We've been working on a new virus to break it down. A virus that could slip through without intimidate detection and bring the whole thing down indefinitely."

"Are you close to having that virus?"

"I think we are. The plan is while Vicki is doing her thing we'll also have some other distraction going on. The hope is that Vicki will have enough time to bring those walls down, but if not at least make a dent for some of us to get through to shut it down remotely. It's still in the works, but we are close. Closer than ever."

"What does Vicki stand for?"

"Nothing. We started with virus names beginning with A."

"Ahh." Riona understood.

After thanking Leo for all he had shown her she was on her way next door, to what Astra had called the Psychic room. She let herself in to see groups doing different things. She watches until she was approached by an older woman.

"I'm Sharon. Are you Riona?"

Riona follows Sharon as she explains what happens in this training room.

"Having this kind of gift is a complex thing. Though most people have one gift of a similar sort, the mind gifts presents itself differently in each person. Some can hold a few gifts of the mind," Sharon tells her.

"Out of everything I've done today this is something that rings most true to me. But, I couldn't tell you why since I haven't figured out what my gift is yet."

Sharon listens to her and to all words she wasn't saying. "Riona, out of all your training you've had today was there anything else you did that did felt just as natural?"

"I really enjoyed helping the injured bird with Kou. I couldn't heal it, but I somehow emotionally connected with it. Like I could sense the pain and it was the best feeling seeing it fly away."

"Riona. I can't tell you where you gonna level in this class yet, but what you've explained so far I think you're in the right place."

Riona looks up at her, eyes full of hope. "Really? This could be my people?"

"It's hard to tell which species you are. These gifts vary greatly. But yes, this could be your family. In any case you're heading in the right direction to figuring things out."

Sharon motions her to sit on the floor as she was, crossing her legs. "If you can sense emotion in the bird let us start there and expand on that. I will seem unemotional outside but I will shift my emotion within. You tell me how I'm feeling."

"I feel more confident I can do that! Everyone's been saying that when I find it I'll just be able to do it, as if it was always there. If this is where I belong then I could see how that might feel."

Closing her eyes Riona breaths rhythmically. When she opens her eyes she would see Sharon in an non-emotional state. She had to find within her the true feeling. But, she found herself trying to steady herself instead. Her own emotions shifting within her, making her head spin. "I'm dizzy."

"Normal at first. You're stretching muscles you haven't used before."

Despite the unpleasant feeling she pushes through it. "I feel- no. It must be you I'm sensing. You are feeling drained. Perhaps... sad?"

"Welcome to the family Riona." Sharon smiles warmly.

Riona rose to her feet with her mouth open. She did it! She found her gift! She could read emotions!

"Riona!" Sharon tries to ground her. "We have a way to go. Most who can read emotions have the potential do so much more! What you've done is a wonderful start."

"What if I can only sense emotions?"

"Then we will work with that. It's a good gift to be able to understand people. I'm here to make sure you're pushing yourself to reach your full potential."

"Thank you!" She rushes back down to the floor, hugging Sharon. For the first time she'd been here she was hugged back.

When Riona left the room she the heard the dinner bell ringing. They day was going by so fast! But she had learned so much!

In the hall, on her way to eat, she had found Leo and Kou and dragged them to the same table to tell them about her findings! She couldn't stop talking. Her friends, Leo and Kou, listens to her.

"I don't know about you guys," Leo stretches in his chair, putting his hands behind is head, "but I've never had click before. I like it."

Now that she was aware of her gift of reading emotions she understood that he meant having them as a group of friends. She liked it too. "Right with ya."

Kou hadn't said anything but was bashfully smiling. Avoiding Leo's gaze. Oh! Riona thought. She understood better. "So, you two never just hung out before?" She was proud of herself for drawing Leo's attention to Kou.

"Well, this place isn't technically the ideal place for clicks and all that. But, I'm down with changing that a little." Leo winks before standing up.

With all in agreement Leo parts from them. Riona couldn't help but give Kou a look afterwards. Kou's rose colored blush on her face told her everything. She didn't have to read her emotional state for that.

When Riona made her way to the combat area River was watching two young men in the ring quietly. When they finished River had nothing to tell them. They must have done what was necessary, Riona thought. Otherwise he would have given them feedback, right?

"I think I'm with you next?" Riona spoke softly, almost questioning it. His demeanor from this morning still lingered in her mind.

He turned his torso slightly, barely looking and tells her to take center.

Center? Oh! Center of the combat ring, right? She walks over hoping she was where he wanted her.

Standing in front of her he tells her, "you're weak. Before I can begin to teach you we need to work on building up your strength. Until then your lesson today is to think outside the box. I'm not going to tell you what you need to do. I need you to figure it out. In any situation you may find yourself will be completely unpredictable. Your mind and body need to learn to adapt and try things you haven't done before. For this lesson you need to break free from your opponent. Got it?"

Riona nods wryly. Trying to understand. Despite not knowing what she would do or what he was planning. Without warning he took a hold of her wrist. She let him pull on it, moving her out of the center position.

"Try to break free from me," he tells her as he continues to pull on her wrist.

Digging her heels in she pulls back on him, but he only tightens his grip. Attempting to take a hold his arm with her other hand she tries to pull his grip downward. His arm lowers but easily withstood her weight. She had no idea what to try expect to pull him back, but he would pull her forward.

"Your opponent is strong. You pulling him back isn't doing anything. You'll only end up hurting yourself. Twist your wrist, positioning your hand to the opening in their hand. On which you can more easily take it back."

Processing his meaning she twists her wrist like he said, jerking it down. She found herself free from his hold. Her wrist slightly red from it.

Before she could blink to think River was reaching out for her other wrist. Once he had it she did what she had done before. Again breaking free. But this time he snatches both her hands. Tugging her away. Keeping a steady foot hold was impossible for her.

Finding herself in this new situations she adjusts herself like he had told her, thinking of new ways to adapt to this situation. Moving just right she broke free from his hold, but lost her balance in the process. Smiling at her success didn't last long.

"Ahh!" Riona straightens up.

Taking advantage of it River took a hold of her pony tale. Not hard, but enough to be noticed. When he spoke there was something in his tone that told her he was less than amused with her taking any kind of pleasure in this.

"You think this is funny?"

Riona's posture caters to the pain. "No. In a real situation like this, most defiantly not." Without thinking she lays her hands on op of his, trying to relax his fingers on her hair.

He tells her to break free from the attack. On repeating it she quickly figures out what to do. Still finding more pleasure in it than she should. She knew she'd shown too much. She saw it in River's face. She didn't know what, but something was off with him. She could sense it.

"If this was real right now you might as well be dead! These lessons could mean your life!"

"I understand." She straightens herself out.

He told her take what she had learned from the top and repeat all the steps. He changed up their stance to keep her thinking, keep her moving, until he added something new. Not seeing it coming he had brought her feet up from under her. Before she knew it she was on her butt.

Hardly knowing what had happened, River came down, sitting on her. Again asking, "what do you do?"

She was finding a pattern in his teaching. Realizing that she had to try to get herself out of it first. Only after her attempt would then tell her what to do.

Unmoved by the advantage of his weight she shifts herself trying to maneuver out of this situation. She couldn't move much but found she could move her feet, so she twisted them around his ankles. On doing that he praises her. She had done something right! She couldn't hide it and smiled. She was trying, she really was, but it set him off again.

River raised her to her feet, pushing her harder. He was moving on her again, flaring his arms at her deflecting blows. But being stronger it only pushed her out to edge. He hands now closing in around her throat.

"What do you do!"

She wasn't sure on this one. Her arms weren't long enough nor strong enough to push him away. Let alone pull his arms away. She was at a complete loss.

"What do you do!"

"I don't know." She shook her head. Clawing at his grip she tries to force his hands away. He only asks the same question.

Looking up at him, seeing his eyes, she couldn't help but try to read him. She needed to understand but what she felt scared her.

With his eyes narrowing something about them were animal like. He would ask her what to do then tighten his hold around her. She was now too lost in fright, trembling at his touch, to try anything more.

"I can't," she whispers. "Please, you're scaring me."

"You should be sacred! You don't know what lies ahead of you."

Her eyes dart up at him. Did he really know what he was doing? He was choking her, hurting her.

"River," her face scrunches up, "stop." Pulling at his hands to let go. "River." Closing her eyes she no longer fights to speak. She intuitively tries to reach him through any possible feeling.

On opening her eyes she saw those around the combat area had stopped to see what was happening, but the expression of their faces told her they were at a loss of what to do. No one moved.

Forcing her mind back on River, she knew they had made some kind of connection before, maybe she could do it again. Keeping her gaze locked on him she spoke in her mind, "River. River. Please." Tears pooling in the corner of her eyes.

River let go abruptly, letting Riona fall over and gasping for air. Coughing slightly her voice went hoarse.

Those standing around seemed to realize that something was out of sorts, but all they could to do was watch. River had turned his back to her, outwardly looking dazed.

Despite what everyone might have been thinking she was compelled to find out what had really happened. If her senses were right there was more than what met the eye. He couldn't have meant what he had done, could he? No.

Leo was stepping off the elevator when he saw the abnormal situation. His gaze fell immediately to Riona. To his eyes she was hurt and no one was doing anything about it. He ran to her side, looking her over. She was breathing heavy. No voice to speak.

He looks up from under his creasing brows. Riv was doing anything but trying help Riona. That was a new low, even for him, Leo thought. Lifting Riona to her feet and guides her to Kou.

"What happened!" Kou rushes to their side. Helping Leo lift Riona onto the bed.

"Riv happened." Leo barked.

"What?" Turning back to Riona she takes a look at the bruised area. There was some discoloration already forming.

"Can't you heal her?" Leo asks.

"Astra said emergencies only. She will heal from this," she explains to Leo.

"Kou. It's Riona. Couldn't you heal her enough to speak to us?"

It didn't take much convincing. Moving her hand around her throat she closes her eyes and begins to give of herself, healing Riona's throat. As the color fades away Riona breathes in a deep, free from any pain.

"I told you," Kou spoke kindly to Riona, "Riv's unpredictable."

Leo shook his head. "He isn't that though. It's something else. I've never seem like this before. Something's gotten into him."

"I agree," Riona finally spoke. "Something more is going on than we can see. That person in the arena that did this- I don't think the real

River would have done this intentionally. I think someone needs to talk to him."

Leo and Kou exchange a look before looking back her. They told her no one would dare to do that. Especially after what happened. That most we're afraid of him.

Riona looks between them in disbelief. "Fine! I'll do it! If River needs a friend, even if he doesn't want it, he can't get rid of me that easily. Not if there's something I can do to help. I'm going to at least try. If I get hurt again I'll have learned my lesson and Kou can patch me up. What's the worst that can happen? He's on our side of this alliance, right?"

Leo scratches his head. "You're crazy, Riona."

"Maybe." Riona smiles. "Hey, she looks at both of them, reaching out to pull them in for a group hug. "Thanks for saving me out there. You two are a great team."

As night was closing in on them, light from the setting sun shone through the windows. Bright enough to still see clearly, but everyone already went their separate ways for evening.

In the midst of the amber glow she saw River standing in the middle of the main floor. As if he was contemplating what had happened earlier. Or, that's what Riona thought he could have been doing. Perhaps he was simply getting ready for his shift.

"River."

"Why are you here?"

"What?" What did he mean by that? Was he referring to standing behind him or at this warehouse with the alliance? "I'm here for my parents."

"Then you should go." River stretches out his arm pointing to the door. "You shouldn't be here." He turns around to face her. "If the only reason is an obligation to someone else then you don't belong here. You don't have what it takes."

"I do!" Riona held her stance against him, but she could feel her eyes starting to burn. He really wasn't wrong. She wasn't strong or smart. But why would he say that? Why was he being so cruel? "River, teach me! I know I can do this if you help me."

"No! You need to leave!"

Riona raises her voice back to him. He couldn't tell her what to do! Especially without explaining himself. Telling her she didn't have what it takes without even trying to train her wasn't a good enough excuse. "This is the only home that I have left!" Tears in her eyes began clouding her vision. "I have no where to go. So tell me! Tell me why you don't want me here! Why you won't help train me so I can cover my own back!"

River looks off into the distance knowing she wasn't going to let this go. "Stupid girl," he says under his breath. Low enough for her not to hear it. "Your name."

"What about my name?" Riona tries to adjusted her tone as well.

"You said your parents said it meant something pure. To me, I compare your name with one who would be fit to be queen. That definition would come with responsibility. You said your parents told you they would always be with you. Yet, they were taken from you. I don't think they meant that in a literal form. I think it meant that both of their gifts got passed down to you. They saw it in you. The potential you had. That you were something pure and something more than both of them. If I'm right on this then it means you're going to hold a lot more responsibility than you realize. It may hold some joy but not without the pain. I don't- I can't see you hurt. Or worse, dead. There may not be enough time to teach you everything you need to know. We don't even know what this war is going to be like. That's why you need to leave before it's too late."

Riona whispers back to him understanding a little better. "Isn't that my choice to make? If Astra saw something in me don't I have the right to try? If everyone starts seeing that I don't have what to takes to be apart of this alliance then you can tell me to walk away. Not before. I have the right to try until then."

River shakes his head. "No. I'm still asking you to leave. This is far bigger than you know. You're done here." River turns his back to leave her there.

"River! Don't you dare walk away! I need you. You can help me! If what you say is true then you know better than anyone how to help me."

River stops in his tracks before walking back to her. Grabbing her arm he physically pulls her with him and pushes her out the door. "Go!"

"River! Stop! I liked you. You were so kind. Why the change?"

River flares his arms out to the side of him. Grounding himself. "I told you why you need to leave this place. So leave and don't come back."

"Why!" Stepping as close as she could to him she holds his stare. "Why?"

"Because of who you are."

Wait, Riona thought. He was going on about her name and what her parents told her about her name. What did he mean that she had both of her parents gifts? How would he know that? Everything he said started sinking in. This wasn't about her name he was worried about. It was who she was. Something she didn't know but he did.

Though River had grabbed a hold of her again, ready to push her out, it seemed as if he saw her thinking and waited for her to form her words.

"River, who am I?"

River looks away from her.

"You know who I am, don't you? And because that, for some reason, you want me to leave. I can feel that from you now. Why are you thinking that this is the only way to protect me?"

River continues to avoid her gaze. Knowing she was trying to peer into him that same way he would to her. He wouldn't be able to hide the truth from her long.

She didn't fully understand but she also felt this inner sense of dread coming from him. As if he was responsible for anything that would happen to her in the future. It was all fuzzy, though.

"River." Riona whispers. "Please." She put her hand on the arm that still had a hold of her. "Who am I?"

Still looking down his jaw quivers slightly, but he decided to reveal it to her. Looking up he tells her, "you're a Visionary."

She scanned his dark brown eyes of truth. Searching for more answers within him. "You're a Visionary too, aren't you?"

He nods.

"You saw my future?"

"When Astra filled me in about you and what she was expecting from you I had what you could say was a vision. A potential future formed. It's not written in stone, but it may as well be. If I know anything about you, you will do whatever it takes, and it might destroy you."

"So Astra does know more about me and parents than she was letting on. If the future is not set in stone then it may as well be malleable. I'm sure you can't tell me what lies ahead of me, but you can help me prepare for such possible outcomes."

"If we did this." His head inches closer than it already was. "If I taught you I don't know if could stand by and watch you-" his words trail off. Trying to be careful how much of the future to expose. "You may be naive and inexperienced, but you got spirit."

"I am naive and inexperienced," she agrees. "That's exactly why I need you." Riona tries to encourage him.

Their noses were so close now they could almost touch, but determined to show that spirit of hers she wasn't going to flinch away. She wasn't about to quit because he saw a partial future for her. "I'm meant to do this. I think you know that. Teach me."

River knew there was no use in throwing her out. If she was to stay then he would have to teach and push her harder than anyone else he had ever taught. This petite and emotional charmed girl will have to change. "It's not a good idea."

"No." She smiles. "We will be a force to be reckoned with."

Before River knew it the side of his lips curved upward. Maybe she could do this. If she could keep that courage upon her. "Stupid girl," he said more lighthearted. "We start tomorrow."

Realizing he was still holding her he gently lets go and she did the same. As he begins to walk away he throws one last comment over his shoulder, "be ready for anything princess."

Watching him go she was grinning, but when he called her princess she was at loss for that meaning. "Princess?" she said aloud. Not realizing he had heard her.

"If you want own up to being a queen you need to start as a princess first."

River's figure now faded into the dark. Only the words of what he said echoed in Riona's mind.

She shook her head. He never ceased to surprise her.

Chapter Five

"You guys! How did we three get put together like this?" Riona questions curiously.

"Come on Riona," Leo says. "You forget your best man over here is a techie? I may have been biased on our grouping for this assignment."

Riona playfully punches him.

"What?" Leo smirks. "Someone said we needed to have more fun around here. This is us having fun!"

"I can't believe they let us get away with it!"

"Hey," Kou interrupts. "did you talk to Riv?"

"Yeah, I did."

"What happened?"

"We talked and yelled but it ended up being a good thing. Everything's good."

"Pfssst," Leo responds. "Yelling I can see. It turning out for the benefit not so much. Are you two like a thing now or something?"

"Ehhh. Something?" Riona teeth cringe into an award smile. "I'm not exactly sure. I was shut up from the world for seventeen years. I'd probably be the last to know if we were."

"You know how old he is? He's like twenty something, right?"

Riona shakes her head at Leo unsure. Did that matter? "But, I found out who I am!"

Kou perks up excitedly for her. "That's great! What species? Did you find your gift?"

"I think I'm a Visionary. I can feel what other people are feeling. That's it, so far. I do have reason to believe my parents were both Visionary's with different sets of gifts. So, it's possible I could acquire both!"

"Dang, look at you." Leo crosses his arms.

Riona wrinkles her nose at him. "I still haven't been able to access them, but you better watch out because I'm coming for you!"

Kou encourages her, telling her she would get there. Initiating them to walk again she presses in close to Riona. "Do you like Riv?"

"I don't know." She looks at her. "Do I?"

Kou tilts her head. "How am I supposed to know?"

"Would it be crazy if I did?"

"Kind of," Kou says hesitantly.

Riona shrugs. "I could always take Leo. If you ever decide to give him up." She looks back at him teasingly.

"Huh?" He pops his head up on hearing his name. "What about me?"

Riona tugs on Kou's arm. "First one back gets Leo!"

"Wait!" Leo catches up with them. When he did he stops them. "Listen."

They all stood silent, listening. Not hearing anything they look around. Still nothing.

"Leo," Riona asks. "What is it?" Riona saw his fingers twitching. A strange color were sparking from them. It looked like electricity. "Are you connecting to something electronically?"

"I can't be. I've always had to be right in front something to manipulate it. But- run!" He pushes them. "Go!"

They start running as fast as they could back to the warehouse door. Leo stops in the doorway, looking out, waiting. Riona saw his hands spark again. That's when she heard it. A buzz sound coming from the distant.

"They're here!" Leo yells. Running to a near by alarm he pulls the lever and the sound begins clamoring through the building.

Everyone jumps into action, shutting everything down. Lights, windows, and doors were all locked up tight. It awoke Riona.

She began to realize how fast things could go down. Was she really ready for that kind of action? "What's going on?" Riona tries to ask. "Is there anything I can do?" She found herself spinning around where she stood until she was facing, "River!"

He took her hand and ran forward. Guiding her around the corner, next to her own room. He pushes her down to the ground. "Stay!"

"What's going on?"

"Rouge Droids!" he yells over his shoulder before running off. Meeting up with Astra. Riona watched as Astra threw a metal something into River's hands. She had one too.

Leo and Kou met Riona where she hid. Sticking close and peaking out from around the corner together.

"What are Rouge Droids?" Riona asks them.

"Rouge Droids are apart of the Rouges high tech," Leo fills her in. "If there's any suspicious activity about any of our alliances, they won't come snooping around themselves, but they'll send those. They can adapt, record, and fire if need be. They are highly sophisticated little things."

Kou continues, "it also means they found something suspicious in this area. We won't be safe here forever in this warehouse. We'll need to find a new hideaway or join another alliance."

"How many alliances are there?"

"They're all around the world as far as I know," Kou answers her.

Riona was just getting used to this place. She wasn't sure what would happen if they had to drop everything to evacuate. Or, what would happen to her.

Last thing she saw was Astra and River on each side of the door, waiting to see what would happen. A slight buzz hummed over the door and everyone kept quiet.

When the sound seemed to fade Astra pulled the door open slowly. There was only a crack of light falling on to the floor which was followed by an extremely bright and violent red burst!

Astra kicks the door open and a single drone came flying in. Once it was inside River kicks the door back closed.

Riona felt herself being pulled back by Leo and Kou. They scooted themselves further into the darkness. Leo whispered to her that the past droids couldn't see in the dark. He could only assume these couldn't either. He also knew he should know better than to assume since the droids were always changing.

The sounds of clanging metal were followed by sounds of the droid shattering on the floor.

Astra's voice calls out, "safe," and the lights above fluctuated before staying on.

Riona, Leo, and Kou came out from behind the hallway corner and saw what was left of droid diced on the floor.

"Leo!" Astra calls out. "Take this thing upstairs and make sure it's disabled for good."

Seeing Astra, Riona felt the time had come for her to catch her up on some things. Astra was still talking to River but she found an opening to make it known she was going to wait to speak with her when she was done.

Astra made it quick with Riv and turns to Riona.

"We need to talk," Riona bluntly tells her with her arms crossed.

Astra raises her brows and motions her to talk.

"You knew who I was all this time and what gifts I could be capable of. You knew my parents. And from the feeling I get, I have some kind of important role in all of this. I want to know more of what my parents roles were here. What their gifts they were, assuming they were both

Visionary's? I need to know what kind of responsibilities you want me taking on. I need to know everything."

"See," Astra said light heartily, "I knew you could figure things out."

Normally Riona would welcome such sarcasm but this was no light matter. She wanted answers.

"Alright." Astra caves under Riona's unblinking stare. "I couldn't tell you who were or what we expected from you. I wanted you to figure that out for yourself. To want it for yourself. We have learned from those still discovering their gifts do better developing them in their own ways. With no obligation or pressure right away. Yes, I knew you were a Visionary. But I really can't tell you what gifts you will inherit. That's something your body will eventually decide. That being said, I do have an idea of what you could be capable of knowing your parents gifts."

"Then they were both Visionary's?"

"Yes. They were both very strong and very controlled in their gifts. The strongest in our alliance. When we came here, they were trained by our previous leader. They then took on a very important mission. They went undercover in a government agency to keep us one step ahead of the game. But it required them to make that role look as real as it could. They were good at it. Together, it was their mission to take on whatever form necessary to keep their back story authentic."

"What did they need to do?"

"They needed to get married."

Riona cocks her head. Thinking of what was being told to her. What it meant. When a image came to mind. She recalled her parents wedding pictures. They hadn't looked as overjoyed as she thought they would have been. "They didn't love each other?"

"No," Astra responds quickly. "Not at first. They were friends. They had a good time in training but they augured a lot too. There was nothing romantic between them. Visionary's do have a very close connection to one another, but they decided to keep some personal boundaries up. They agreed to marriage out of the importance and success of the mission. Of course, as they grew into the role of this mission, they got closer. Naturally, as they needed to rely and trust on one another during this isolated time. When their friendship based walls between them dissolved they took the time to really see each other for who they were. They started to notice the closer they got, even if it was as friends at first, that their connection made their gifts stronger. This is something that has never been seen in our culture before. Over time they did fall in love. Something they never thought would happen and then they had you. I never saw them more happier. Somehow, with both of their gifts combined, they saw something in you as a baby. That you had the potential to be stronger than both of them. No one here has ever been as strong as they were with their gifts. Imagine if you possessed both."

"I hope that's true Astra, but I don't feel very connected to my gifts yet. It's like they're right there but I can't access them fully. Sharon says-"

Astra cuts Riona short and continues, "during one attack our leader was injured and eventually died. Your parents became the ones to oversee this place. They helped to train others as our late leader did. Until they stepped back to take care of you. Yet, with every precaution taken to keep your family safe the Rouges still found them. The point is, Riona, we may be safe in this warehouse for now, but there's no hiding forever once you're on the Rouges radar. I took over your parents position and I've been running around like crazy trying to stay on top of things. It wasn't suppose to be my place, but for now it is. That running will not stop until we stop the Rouges. That was my choice to continue on. So, you need to understand if you decide to join this fight, there's no going back. We need you, but I also need you to understand the risks. Only you know what you're capable of. I need you to honestly ask yourself if you can do this. I trust you'll make the right choice. Even if it's to leave."

"Astra, you have a team to help you. Giving those the right responsibility will help you. Make use of it while you have it. Make use of me."

"You are your mothers daughter."

Her tone had Riona questioning what Astra said. "You two were close?"

"Yeah kid, we were. Your mother is my sister."

Riona expression fell stiff. How had she not known? Why didn't her parents tell her they had family? The more she came to know the more she realized she didn't know. How many secrets were left to uncover?

"You must understand," Astra began, "they never told you out of protection."

Riona coughed up a laugh. "You're my aunt Astra!" As hard hitting as that was, she was starting to get used to these secret surprises.

"Oh dear god. You do not have to formalize that, let alone call me that."

Although appearing cold, Astra was warmed by the gesture. She winced slightly when Riona stole a hug from her but she stood there allowing it.

"Alright kid, that was nice, but listen to me now. I heard things didn't go well with Riv last night. I did hear his concern for you the other day about your safety, but he will have to deal.'"

"Oh, I know. We talked it out."

Astra hug her mouth open mid sentence. "You guys talked? Like verbalizing actual words to sentences?" She pushes her head forward trying to understand.

"Ahhh. Yeah. Something like that. It was enlightening for sure."

"So, you guys have this all sorted out?"

"I think so."

"Hmm." Astra made a noise in her throat. "Well good. I was going to tell you that though his training maybe be odd, he is one of the best trainers and most powerful in his gift that we have here currently."

Riona squints at her. "River is?"

"I have very high hopes for the both of you. Maybe you'll be our next legends, like your parents."

"Are you expecting us to..."

"Be unstoppable."

"Oh." Riona chuckles uncomfortable. "Right."

"Now get to work!" Astra pushes her forward. "He's waiting for you."

"What?" Riona looks over her shoulder to find River standing near the ring waiting for her. "Oh." Looking back at Astra she smiles at her. "See you around aunt Astra!"

Astra rolls her eyes but almost looked amused before walking away.

Riona spins on her heel and walks to where River was standing. "Waiting on me?"

River shrugs.

"I know training is important and everyone is working hard, but I have a request. Do you think we can get out of here? Go somewhere? Anywhere. This is the only time I will ever ask this. I promise! I need to sort all this stuff in my head, you know. Everything's been a lot to process. Everything I thought I knew, it's-"

He slide his eyes over from his unmoved head to look at her. It was an odd request, but valid. Not something he expected, though. "Us?"

"Yeah, why not?"

"Alright," he agrees. "I know a place. Be prepared to put those muscles to use. You're not getting out of training that easily." He walks past her leaving her behind. On her realization they were leaving right now he hears her scurrying after him to keep up.

The evening skies were turning to a lavender haze as they walked past a few abandoned buildings. They kept close to the woods until they came up to a contraption in the trees. Equipped with a pull rope.

"Get in."

Standing in the make shift lift River hands Riona a rope as he took a hold of the other.

"We're going to pull ourselves up?" She looks at him wide eyed.

River raises his eyebrows.

"Oh, okay." She gathers a tighter grip on the rope. She found it wasn't quite as hard as she thought, but she did still had to use all that she had to do it.

They pulled themselves up into the trees until they were hidden in the leaves. Everything else below started to look small. "How did you know this was here?"

"I made it. It's my get away place to think when things start to get overwhelming. The weight of waiting and hoping this war could be over can be hard."

"Do you think it's soon? Especially if I somehow play a part in this war?"

"Maybe. I push everyone so hard to be the best version of themselves to be ready. I often wonder if I'm ready. I have my gift to foresee as well as my physical ability to fight, but it never feels like it's enough." He pauses, looking somewhere far away. "Why I'm telling you this, I don't know."

"Can I say something?"

"Nothing's stopped you before."

"I think you have more to your gift than you realize."

"Is that so?" River sits down, waiting to hear what she has to say about it.

"It's possible I have two gifts," Riona follows his lead and sits as well, "so what if you do, too? What if that longing for something more and not feeling enough is pushing you to find that within you? Whether it be an expansion of your current gift or an addition to another one."

River's eyes widen. Entertaining the thought that he had something more to give.

"Let me show you." Reaching out to take his hand she sets it on her shoulder. "You said you can foresee, but what can you see or feel within me?"

No one had ever dared to tell him what to do, except Astra. He was good with that, so this was new for him. Hand on her shoulder he adjusts himself slightly before closing his eyes to breathe. Connecting to her emotions. "You feel at peace."

"See, you do have more gifts then you realize." Riona smiles at him. "Do you feel emotions that someone else may have a hard time feeling? Or, feel emotions one is trying to hide?"

"What do you, someone who has so much to say, have to hide?" he says studying her closer.

Instead of looking away, she looks up at him, telling him to read her again. She hadn't meant to imply anything, but since it came up she had to know.

Same as before River closes his eyes, focusing once again. It was distracting to sense her outside presence watching him, but he was still able to reach a kind of wonder and curiosity within her. The feeling pulls him in. Her pure heart and her gentle disposition was accompanied by- His eyes pop open. It wasn't what either of them thought was hiding in the flow of emotions.

River's reaction confirmed Riona's suspensions. Hoping the shade from the trees were enough to hide her growing blush. "If I'm right about you having multiple gifts, let's try one more thing. The gift of giving." Riona stares at their feet. "Give me the courage to do something about this. It would prove the theory since we both know I don't have that kind of courage." She bites her inner lip uncertain. "Only if you want."

River closes his eyes a moment before peeking out with one eye.

Riona giggles. "I don't feel anything!"

"I was just testing you."

"On what?" Her eyes widen. "You know I don't have that kind of courage! That's the point. If I'm right about you on this, if you can give, share, or manipulate ones emotions this will prove that."

He shifts himself. "Okay." Closing his eyes his hands rise. Hovering at each side of her head and closing in.

Watching him focus she sees his eyebrows twitching but didn't feel any transfer of courage from him. She was sure he could do this, but maybe she was making too much out of it. Being able to foresee and feel was amazing gifts. Perhaps she got too excited at the possibilities. Starting to doubt herself she felt a wave of sadness building up within her.

With River's hands floating around her hair she closes her eyes. If there was any chance he could hear her she told him in her mind, "River. It's okay. You are enough."

At that moment both his hands clutch the sides of her head. The suddenness of it made her gasp. Her eyes opened briefly but fell shut again. On doing so something was bubbling inside her. A feeling she wasn't well acquainted with. Courage!

Opening her eyes, it was undeniable what had been done. What she had sensed was true! River clearly had many gifts! Possibly more. She still had yet to know if he could hear her in his mind.

Riona smiled brightly at him as he let her go. She liked how it felt. If only she could keep it! With that newfound courage, barely thinking, she reaches out. Putting a hand in River's hair she closes the space between them and fills it with a feather like touch across his lips.

On pulling away she saw him smile! A smile with teeth. She didn't know he had an expression like that. She was in awe of it. Competently distracted by it until she felt his hand at the back of her head guiding her back to him.

After parting she raises her eyes up at him, whispering, "whatever gifts you have will be enough for this war. This kind giving of yourself could be vital. It might be what we need to give the Rouges a chance to change their mind and to help those on the earth with no knowledge of what's been happening come to clarity. You can give them that and so much more."

River rests his forehead on hers. "Is that my courage talking?"

"You simply gave me the courage to say it."

From that moment on Riona's training intensified. She trained with River to get herself stronger and trained with Sharon to grow into her gift. Taking it all in with seriousness and responsibility. Even going above and beyond she learned more about everyone's gifts in the warehouse. How Kou healed to what Leo could do with his gift in connection to anything technical. Riona learned and in turn helped them strengthen their gifts, too. Sensing only more and more what they were all capable of. Including herself.

Chapter Six

With her weapon in hand Riona circles. She wasn't sure if their training was truly fair now that they could predict each others upcoming move. If anything it only pushed them to be more spontaneous and unpredictable.

As River went after a opening Riona turns her weapon around in time to catch his blow. The metal echoing in warehouse on impact. They continue this until Riona's hand slips from sweating.

With another vulnerable opening River hits her weapon out of her hands. This would test her on what she would do next. They had not specifically trained on this but he had faith in her ability to adapt.

Bending back Riona kicks, knocking his weapon away from him as well. Both defenseless she knew River was testing her. He always did. Unlike the first time she trained with him she was now prepared. She was only briefly taken by surprise when River pressed on more intensely.

River, of course, knew her weakness and got her with it every time. She really needed to watch her feet! Riona, now laying on her back jumps back up before he could hold her down. They had done this many times before but this time, instead of holding her down, his hands went to her throat. It was the first time he did that since he had unintentionally hurt her.

Tensing slightly under his touch she couldn't help but remember it. This time it didn't hurt, but something inside her churned. She tries to calm herself to think clearly.

It was all apart of her training and she knew River was in complete control of himself. She needed to know how to get out of this, but something inside her was telling her she was in real danger. The feeling was raising too rapidly to extinguish.

River saw it in her mind. What she was thinking. What she was feeling. He loosened his grip even more to assure her that he was in control, as she already knew. He could never apologize enough for what had happened. And he wouldn't blame her if she couldn't trust him fully after that. Right now he was only trying to do what he thought was best for her in the long run, despite the fear of it. But, while waiting out her emotions he could feel something inside her changed.

She was staring at him when her bright blue eyes began turning and glowing gold. Wide eyed and confused things around them began shaking. Loose items became airborne and quickly moved toward River. He moves and ducks as weapons from the walls, targets, and any lose items came at him.

When the moving items came to a halt he looked back at Riona. Her eyes were fading back to blue. Soon after her eyelids closed she began tipping over. River rushed to catch her in time.

Riona was resting in his arms on the floor when she came to. "Are you hurt?" She abruptly sits up.

He looks at her curiously. "No." He shook his head.

"I hardly knew what I was doing. I'm so sorry!"

"I may not understand what you did, but it was powerful. Don't fear that gift within you."

Riona shakes her head. "No, I'm never doing that again. I felt like I was trapped in fear. I could have hurt you."

River holds her steady. "Riona. You opened yourself to another gift. Uncertainty in how to use it is natural. Talk to Sharon about it. She can help you." He strokes her hair, trying to calm her. "You did good."

On looking up Riona saw the other trainees staring at her, watching her. "They're afraid of me," she whispers.

"No." He shakes his head. "No. Look at me." He turns her head back to him by her chin. "They are looking up to you. You have too much of a caring soul to hurt anyone. They're not afraid of you. I'm not afraid of you. Don't be afraid of yourself."

Her eyes hastily searched his. "You tried to prevent me from following this course. You wanted to protect me from getting hurt, but what if it's me that you need to be afraid of? Is it possible that this gift is a dangerous gift? That it's too big for me to harness and control? Maybe you were right on insisting that I leave."

With both hands on her face, he kept her focused, "you are not dangerous. The only danger here are the Rouges. I am not afraid of you. Don't you dare think such things. You hear me? I got you."

If he was right then why did she feel so hopeless in controlling what she felt? She could have hurt him! With tears in her eyes she felt a warmth enfolding around her. Holding on tight she tries to stifle her cries.

When Riona saw Sharon she explained everything that happened and how she felt about it.

"Remember the first time you threw your knife? You weren't able hit the target's middle right away. But after some time and practice you were able to hit it every time. Your gifts that are emerging are no different. The more you use that muscle the more control you have." Sharon hands her three soft handheld balls. Directing Riona to move them upward from her.

Riona holds them. Trying to use her mind to tell them what she wanted them to do. Slowly the colored balls in hand start shaking slightly before they lifted into the air.

"Good Riona! Good!" Sharon praises her.

Riona breathes a sign of relief. Maybe Sharon was right. Maybe River was right. She was currently moving the round objects in the air in a small circle, becoming more comfortable in that ability, but soon they began shaking. "Sharon?"

"Set them down gently, dear. That's enough for today. The muscles in that gift are weak. We have to build the strength needed-"

Without warning, before Riona could fully let the balls go, she felt herself losing control. The balls flew across the room in all directions. "Ah!"

"It's okay, my dear."

"But I lost control! Complete control! Is that not concerning?"

Sharon gave her a bright and reassuring smile. "We will continue to work on it. Riona, your gifts are beautiful. Treat them as such."

After her lesson with Sharon Riona went back downstairs to find River.

"That's good news."

"Maybe."

"Riona, I've been meaning to tell- wait." River stops, tilting his chin upward.

"What did you see? What happened? You had a vision, didn't you?"

When he snaps out of it he squeezes her arm. "They're coming!"

Before she knew it he threw her the weapon they were fighting with earlier and he ran to ring the bell. Immediately after everyone started moving about. Doing what was needed to prepare. Astra appears to help, taking up her weapon as well.

Riona found herself next River on one side of the main floor while Astra held down the other. Waiting for the droids to arrive.

The quietness made the atmosphere seem loud and intense. Hearing her own breathing she tries to keep it in check. Under the door shadows moved about. Aside from that there were no other signs they were in danger.

Stttz.

"They've found us!" Astra yells.

Riona looks between River and Astra. What would they do if the Rouges won? Before she could contemplate it further the door was opened wide and the droids hovered inside.

The three of them went after the Rouge droids. One by one destroying them, while staying clean of their laser bursts. When all the droids were broke and steaming on the ground Astra flips the lights back on.

"If they sent more than one they're beyond suspicions and they'll keep sending more until one of these return to them. We need to evacuate." Astra hesitates a moment. Knowing what had to be done. She didn't like it but it was the only way to protect them all. "Proceed with code nine! We need to get out of here. Go!"

Before Riona's eyes everyone in the warehouse started moving quickly. What's was code nine? She froze not knowing what to do. "River!" Where was River?

"Code nine is an abort plan." River snuck up behind her and kept her moving. "Everyone here is assigned a safe way out to a near by alliance if we we're ever compromised. Assigned by small groups or pairs of two."

"What about me? I didn't know! I don't have-"

River stops to look at her. "Me! Let's go!" He takes a hold of her hand and leads them to the door.

Riona had no idea she was paired up with him in case of emergency evacuation. Wide eyed she looked back this place in action. But wait! "What about Kou and Leo? Astra!"

"They can take care of themselves. They all have their own escape plans. If we knew everything it would create more risk. Trust the plan. Trust Astra. Trust me."

Before Riona let River take her out she looked back. She saw Leo and Kou with backpacks on. They were hand in hand leaving together. Oh! They got paired together!

They caught her looking at them before their departure. They smiled and nodded to her.

Riona nodded back. Giving them one last smile in case she would never see them again.

"Okay, let's go," Riona tells River.

Outside they could hear the humming of more droids on their way. By now the warehouse was nearly evacuated. All of the alliance broke into groups or pairs and they ran off in all different directions.

River and Riona ran behind the warehouse and straight into the woods. Occasionally looking behind to make sure they weren't followed.

Riona hoped all those defending themselves would be okay, but she couldn't deny that some may have to fight their way out.

When the sound of humming got louder Riona spun around in time to see a Rouge Droid flying towards them, targeting River.

"River, behind you!"

It was as if he had already anticipated the attack. He snatched up a near by stick from the ground in time to hit the droid head on. The Rouge Droid was now shattered on the ground. It was then a few more came around the corner.

Riona scans the ground where she stood but all she had was rocks. Picking them up frantically she prepares herself when two Rouges Droids picked up her movement. Bouncing, she waited until she knew she couldn't miss.

Spzzzt! Spzzzt! The Rouges Droids fired.

Dodging them she throws the rocks, hitting them both. One went down while the other only lowered slightly before moving back toward her to shoot again. Throwing another rock in hand she takes the Rouge Droid out for good.

River ran back to help her. But he came to see she had done it, rather successfully, herself. Stopping suddenly he smiles, "good work princess."

"Ahh." She breathed rapidly from the adrenaline. "Just give me the crown already."

"Riona!" River saw another Rouge Droid flying after them and picked up a few rocks. He threw them at the Rouge Droid as it fired. Taking it out with ease. "Okay, come on!" He reaches out to her. What River did not see was that the fire from the Rouge Droid ricocheted off a near by tree, hitting Riona.

"Riona? Riona!" He runs to her. "Talk to me Riona." What he saw was something he had not foreseen and he panicked.

"Ugh." Riona stood holding her side. When she lifted her hands she saw her own blood.

River wondered why he didn't see this coming. This wasn't supposed to happen! Not like this. Not this soon. This wasn't in his dreams. "Riona." He picked her up under the knees. "Stay with me."

Riona barely knew what had happened before she realized she was hurt. With her system in shock she fell unconscious into River arms.

Chapter Seven

On opening her eyes Riona didn't recognize where she was, but the smell of smoke lingered in the air as she shifts her head to look around. She was enclosed in some kind of material. Staring at the top, where it came together, she cocks her head. A tipi?

Pushing herself to sit up she gasps. Her hands sprung to her side. Remembering what had happened at the sudden sensation of pain.

She hadn't known pain like this before. Not at this intensity. Her body didn't know how to process it. Inching herself to sit upward she groans. In attempting to pull herself up she realizes she wasn't wearing her clothes, but was wearing a tan nightgown. No, not a nightgown. Riona tried to understand. Where was she? Where was River?

Despite what she was wearing she lifted her clothing up to look at the wound. It was bandaged up neatly. Had she done this and not remembered, or did River do this?

Carrying herself gently she walked to what seemed to be the opening of the tent. Pulling it back she saw more tipis. And those walking about were wearing similar clothing to what she had on. Wait, she thought. This was a Native American camp?

She had learned about different cultures from her parents. She also remembered her parents telling her how Native Americas used to live, but she didn't think they lived that way anymore.

Her eyes focused on those working in their gardens using simple tools as a few women passed by her carrying woven baskets. Others tended to the fires. Her mind was all too foggy that she hardly heard her name being called out. Was she dreaming?

Turning toward the voice she found herself in a hug. Oh! Realizing who it was she hugs River back.

"How are you feeling?" he asks, pulling back to look at her.

"Umm. A bit disoriented. You'll have to fill me in on everything."

A man came to their side. An older face that had aged with grace. He lay a hand on Riona's shoulder. "It's good to see you awake." The man then turns to set a hand on River. "Go get us something to eat Ziibi. I'm sure the girl is hungry."

Riona looks between them in confusion. What did he call River? The look was clearly evident. Yet, the command made River waver. She sensed he didn't want to leave her, but he nods to the old man before heading off.

"Yes, father."

Before Riona could digest that, the older man put his hand on her, guiding her. She sat on a soft like stool around the fire. Was he really River's father?

"I'm sure you have many questions."

"I do." Riona nods.

The older man looked around her, almost as if he was waiting to see River return. But he continues talking.

"My name is Niigaanii. Leader over this camp."

"I didn't realize there were places still like this."

"Long story short we were able to acquire this land here to keep somethings traditional. Doing all of this works in our benefit to keep the Rouges from sniffing us out. We look harmless."

"Rouges? You're with the alliance?" Everything became clearer.

Niigaanii leans in close with a mischievous smirk on his face. "For many years no one has ever known that."

Riona shook her head taking it all in with awe. She had so much to learn!

"He cares for you," Niigaannii interrupted her thoughts.

"What?" She looks at him contemplating his meaning.

"He has never really cared for anything. He does what is needed for the future of all people, but he has never cared so deeply as he does for you."

"How do you know that?"

"A father knows his son. I may not be as powerful as he is but I can see a few things in you too, you know."

"You're a Visionary?"

"I assume as much. When I found Ziibi at the river it wasn't a coincidence. He was a baby crying out for help. I wasn't anywhere near this river and I heard him in my mind. Yet, I somehow knew where to find him."

"Does Ziibi mean river?"

Niigaannii nods slowly. "Do you care for River as he does you?

Looking down bashfully she begins to think of everything he'd done for her. She couldn't have done it without him. Now, she couldn't imagine him not being beside her. Up until this point they've helped and guided one another. "Yes, I suppose I do."

"You two were meant to be together. I can see that much."

Soon after that conversation River came back with a couple plates of food. Both of them making sure Riona sufficiently ate before talking again.

"My daughter. What is the meaning of your name?"

"Riona? I've been told it had multiple meanings. Pure. Perhaps queen."

"Perhaps? Niiaagnii raised his brows. "No perhaps. You have a heart of a queen, no doubt."

Riona smiles at that reply before stealing a look at River sitting next to her. He turns to her the same time. Both in connection. Both in perfect understanding.

Niigaannii, sitting across from them, observers everything about them with a all knowing smile. "My daughter. You must have more questions. What would you like to know?"

"What do you know about the Rouges? I haven't heard much besides they're controlling all of this."

He nods. "Legend tells, over the generations, that they were ones who claimed they did not have any particular gift. And yet they were especially smart. They could create anything they put their minds to. But, because most species around them had a visible gift, they started to feel threatened. They became paranoid that the gifted species could take control over them. What was a misguiding thought turned into a war and the result is what you see today. They have nothing on us expect their technology to keep us caged. Sadly, they created the enemies they we're afraid of. Themselves. We're just planning to take back was rightfully ours. What was ours was theirs too. They simply refuse to see that."

"I can't believe that's what started all of this. Talk about overthinking. I wonder if there's any way to give them clarity?"

"At this point in time," River spoke up, "there's no use in giving them pity. They can stop this if they wanted."

"River is right, Riona. But that heart of yours is in the right place."

Riona smiles before nodding. She wanted to believe there was good in all things, but she knew some things were beyond saving and hoping in. She just hated to think that way.

Niigaanii stood up slowly before taking up her hands. "I know you just got up but evening is setting in. Your body will do good with trying to get some rest." Niigaanii rested his warm hand on her shoulder before moving to River. With his hand on the side of River's face he looked so proud as he smiled at his son.

Scooting to the edge of her seat Riona caters to the pain. Until her accident she had no idea how dedicate human flesh was. Even strength had its limits. She placed her feet firmly on the ground to stand when she realized she was being lifted up instead. With a little help from River. If he hadn't, she wouldn't have made it onto her feet herself.

Supporting her weight River walks them back to the tipi. The ground of the tipi was well cushioned with quilts and blankets. That being the case River prepares where she would sleep. Making it as comfortable as he could for her.

She began to bend down onto her bedding but she couldn't stop herself from moaning from the movement. She hadn't expected the pain to feel worse as time went on.

"Here." River places his hand on her upper back. "Abdominal wounds are the worst for moving about. Lay against my hands and I'll lower you down."

To her surprise it was nearly pain free. Adjusting comfortably she felt a sensation rushing over her. Confused her body began shaking. Shivering as if she was cold.

River lifts the quilt over her. It was if he had done this before. Taking care of the wounded was something he seemed to know well. It made Riona curious.

He explains to her, "your body is recovering. It's still trying to figure out what to do as it heals. Being tired doesn't help the shakes. Try to relax. The shakes should even out."

"O-okay."

After River finished adjusting Riona he takes a thinner blanket and spreads it out. Riona watches him as he takes a seat on it, not too far from where she was.

"Staying?" That was all her quivering lips could manage to say.

He stretches himself out on the ground, his hands behind his head. "Your vulnerable. I'm not going anywhere."

Okay, she thought. Almost as if telling him telepathically. She still wasn't completely sure he could hear her, but it felt right somehow.

Trying to keep calm and breathe her shivering eventually stopped and she fell asleep. When Riona's eyes opened next she wasn't quite sure of the time, but she already felt better. The pain was manageable and her energy had seemed to have returned.

Twisting her head to the side, through groggy eyes, she saw River stirring about. His sleep was restless. Cautiously, she pushes herself up with her hands. Looking at River more clearly she sees him drenched, shifting about, and frantic.

"River," she whispers. "River!" Throwing the quilt off she crawled to his side. "Let me see."

And with that a wave of intense emotion suddenly came down upon her. Feelings of fear, worry, and the inability to help. "Let me see," she whispers again.

With that sights of a burning red fire with sounds of screams engulf her. She caught glimpses of those fighting around her. Among them she sees herself. She watches as her own eyes open, the color of them changing to gold, before screaming.

"River!" Riona put her hands on him. "River, wake up!"

Opening his eyes he drew back from her before realizing what was going on. Laying his head back down he covers his face.

"You had a nightmare."

"I keep seeing it over and over like it's written in stone."

"What's written in stone?"

His hands on his face tighten. Almost already regretting what he would tell her. "Your death."

Her death? What she saw was her death? Confused and longing for more information was all over her face.

He sat up, facing her. "It's not too late to change your mind. We could run away."

"No!"

"Riona, listen. All have to go on is knowing that you might die in an explosions of Rouge Droids during the war. Something's can't be changed or altered. I can't," he trails off. Placing his hand on the side of her neck. "I can't lose you. Not now."

Riona scans his face. He really had seen something about her future. That she couldn't deny. From the very start he wanted to protect her from that future. But he still agreed to help her prepare even with knowing where it might lead. Now, that possible future had became more real each and every day. And every day he became more scared of losing her.

The suggestion to run was certainly tempting, but Riona knew that their personal feelings were clouding their judgment. Could they really drop everything they worked so hard for and run away? No, she thought. They came too far. She knew that. He knew that.

They needed to keep their journey in the forefront of their minds. To remember why they were doing this, why they trained, and why they needed each other to succeed. She didn't know what would happen in the future, but it didn't change her hope that things would turn out alright. That in end, they would be alright too.

Hand on his face she allowed River to read her answer in her expression and feelings. Even if, for the briefest of moments, she really wished they could run away. But, how would the outcome of implementing Vicki change if they weren't there? They were to vital to the plan. She couldn't let Astra, Leo, Kou, and everyone else down. They all made their sacrifices. Unfortunately, this was theirs.

If this upcoming war would mean her death, it pained her more than anything to think they couldn't be together. Not in the way it might actually matter. But, because of their sacrifices many others, for generations to come, would be able to have their happy endings.

Reaching out to her and scooting her closer River rests his forehead on hers before slowly nodding in approval. Riona wanted to say so much, but choking on her words she looks up at him instead. Allowing herself to get caught up and fall into his hickory colored eyes. Who would have known they held so much feeling. That this man, once cold in appearance, was so warm.

It was as if they were of one mind when they came together. Moving every so gently, every so slowly, just in case it would be their last kisses shared.

"I'm not going anywhere. You hear me? I'm right here." Riona tucks her head under his chin. "I'm right here," she said, squeezing him tight.

She continued to repeat the words over and over in her mind thereafter, "I'm right here, River. I will always be here."

That's when she felt his arms tighten around her. It took her by surprise slightly. Maybe. Maybe he could hear her! But nothing would surprise her more than when she heard him respond back to her telepathically.

"I know."

Chapter Eight

At midday River and Riona stood near the bustling water as they communicated with Astra through their watches.

"It's good to hear you're both safe. You're probably in one of the safest alliances there is. Stay put for now. We have a team inside The White House keeping an eye on things. It looks like we're getting close to implant the virus. We will call everyone in by then. It shouldn't be long now."

The inside job was something Riona recognized as the job her parents had. She knew it was a dangerous job. Who did they choose to send this time?

"Can we help in anyway?" Riona asks.

"No. You're still healing. We need you to be in top shape for later. Leo and Kou have this under control."

Leo and Kou? They sent Leo and Kou on the inside! With wide eyes she looks up at River, who only furrows his brows.

"Thanks Astra. Riv out."

Riona's worried thoughts for her friends her were abruptly interrupted when she felt a hold on her wrist. Stopping her unconscious pacing.

"They'll be fine. You know they're strong as well as gifted." River tries to assure her.

"I know. I just can't get what happened to my parents out my head. I can only imagine what would happen if they got caught."

"They won't. Circumstances are different and they don't have a family to worry about."

"You're right." She had to trust they knew what they were doing. "Thanks."

Intertwining his fingers with hers he leads them back to camp. "C'mon princess."

Back at camp they saw the layout of things had changed and everyone was gathering about.

"What's going on?" Riona watches the commotion.

"Ah."

"What?"

"She's back."

"Who?"

That's when Riona saw many hovering over a couple with their newborn baby in arms when Niigaanii approached them, filling Riona in.

"That is my daughter Memengwaa with her new family." He gestures. "They were away for a little bit, but now they're back. They came home to have another, more traditional, wedding with friends and family here."

"Oh! How wonderful!" Riona reaches out gave Niigaanii a hug to congratulate him.

"Come," Niigaanii motions. "It will start as soon as they're ready. It wont be long." He glances back to look at Riona. "Pay attention my daughter. It may soon be your turn," he tells her before returning to his grandchild.

Gah! Riona turns her head bashfully. Except Niigaanii didn't stay to see her reaction. Instead, she felt more exposed from the thought Niigaanii planted in her mind. Well knowing that the person standing behind her could hear her thoughts.

There was no use in trying to hide. They were Visionary's. They technically could hold back from using such gifts of the mind, but they couldn't hide anything from each other even if they wanted to. Plus, they had already mutually decided to open themselves fully to one another without reservations.

Except, they never took the time to just talk about them. Really, what was there to talk about when you don't know what tomorrow will bring? They weren't even sure they would get their happy ever after. So, entertaining the thought of them marrying in the future never crossed her mind before now.

The word marriage sounded so odd, so adult, after all. She wasn't sure if she felt like an adult herself. Yet, the idea of him becoming her family was enough to make her think and blush. With her cheeks tinted pink her and her eyes under her browns she peers at River shyly.

His face was formed into a partial smile with his brows raised, clearly teasing her. The color drained from her face from the expression. It completely threw her. Perhaps, that's exactly why he did it.

Her surprise gave him some amusement. Smiling one of his rare smiles with his teeth he pulled her head close, kissing her temple, before leading her with him.

When the ceremony started Memengwaa was dressed in a traditional Native American wedding attire. She and her husband stood in front of them all while Niigaanii took the lead.

"Who is it she's marring?"

"That's Moving Water. He's apart of the Aqua species. He can swim and live under water if he wanted. His gift of manipulating water got him his name."

"He's a merman?"

River muffles his chuckle behind his fit, pretending it was a cough. "Something like that," he whispers into her ear.

"What about your sister Meg-waa?"

"Memengwaa? Her name means butterfly. My adoptive mother was a Farillia. So, Memengwaa has the ability to fly."

"The baby?"

"Who can say? A winged mermaid?"

Hiding her uncontrollable laughter in River's shoulder she tries to watch as Niigaanii motions something with his arms. Soon, some of the family approach the couple with a hand made quilt in their hands. They covered them in the quilt, wrapping it over their shoulders.

"This quilt," Niigaanii turns the couple to face those watching, "represents that two will form into one."

Riona leans herself into River, whispering again, "that was really cool."

After the ceremony was over those who had drums started banging them in celebration of the joining of the two. Riona, in awe, kept looking over at River to make sure he was still paying attention. He may have experienced his before but she hadn't! River's fingers moved her hair out of her face, tucking it behind her ear to see her expressions better. Riona, now meeting his gaze, gave him the brightest smile.

All Riona knew, right now, was that she was never happier. All worried thoughts about tomorrow were forgotten. She wanted to live everyday like this. The uncertain future would come eventually, but until then she was determined to never take one second she had with River for granted. Plus, she still had to tell him that she loved him, but chances were he already knew.

He did. River always heard it, even if it wasn't explicitly stated. Once they fully opened that gift between them, it kept getting stronger. At times they had to differentiate what were her thoughts and what were his, but they were getting the hang of it.

With a aching heart he smiles back at her. His worries for the future often gnawed at him. It was the one the thing that he tried to hide from her. But, in regard to how he felt for her. That he could not hide. He had fallen in love with her too.

Chapter Nine

While River and Riona were safe in their alliance Leo and Kou had a very important mission from inside The White House. This mission was to make sure that no one, the Rouges or government officials, got wind of their upcoming plans to distribute the virus. The last thing they needed was anyone preventing them from reaching their goal. This plan was the only way they knew to try to free everyone from this caged world...

Headlights from passing cars illuminated their faces in brief instances. In the front seat the taxi man looks into the mirror, seeing Leo and Kou sitting in the back seat. "We're almost there! You two really have a break of lifetime!"

"Awe, thanks Chet!" Leo responds.

Leo sits up straighter knowing they were close. Kou had been resting on him, but she re-positioned herself as well. Leaning over, Leo put his mouth near her ear, "we've gotten everyone fooled so far." The corner of his lips curve up mischievously. "This mission will be a breeze."

Kou, doing her best to put on the same smile, reaches for a fallen strand of Leo's hair. "I really do have to get Astra back for this. Making you my pretend fiancé and all."

"You ready to sell the performance?" Leo winks at her. "Once we go in there's no going back."

"I think you're having too much fun, dear."

"We're going to The White House! Why not have a little fun with it? Before you know it it'll be over and we can go back to being friends."

It is true Kou viewed Leo as a friend with the idea of something more. But, if he always a tease in a relationship, fake or not, then she couldn't wait for it to be over.

"Here we are!" the taxi driver exclaimed.

Being escorted inside they walked through the long hallways and high ceilings before coming to an elevator. It took them up a few floors before the door opened. Not too far down the hallway the man ahead of them turns to face a door.

"This will be room during your stay." He opens it for them. "Please, make yourself comfortable. You will be informed of your meeting with the President in the morning. Have a goodnight."

Leo and Kou peer into the room from the door way. What they observed was a far bigger room than either of them were used to at the alliance.

"It makes sense we'd sharing a room," Kou says to herself.

"Shh." Leo leans in to her smiling.

Even before she had a chance to blush a quick peck came across her lips.

"Cameras," he whispers to her.

Kou knew he was right. Now that they were here they could not break character. They couldn't afford to. But that kiss, barely a kiss, made her fingers rise to her lips remembering what was there.

Shutting the door behind them she scans the room again, taking it all in. Being inside somehow made it seem more spacious. Even the bed was bigger than either of them had ever seen. Surely, it was one of a kind.

Leo, who was already making himself at home, stole a pillow from the under the sheets. He fluffed it out and drops it on the couch. Stretching himself on it he tucks his arms behind his head and closes his eyes.

"What happened to staying in character?" Kou asks.

"Eh. No cameras in here. I checked. The bed is all yours," Leo replies without looking at her.

Kou couldn't tell if he was really as comfortable on the couch as he made it look, but perhaps they would switch out every night to make it fair.

After dressing in the bathroom Kou climbs onto the bed and found her way into the covers. "Goodnight Leo," she said as she laid her head down. But the way she could hear him breathing told her he was already sleeping.

Early the next morning there was a knock at the door before either of them were awake. Kou lifts her head to listen, making sure she wasn't dreaming. The sound came again. Throwing off the covers she shuffles to the floor and opens it without thinking.

"Good morning. I have-"

The man stops short seeing Leo sleeping on the couch. A look of confusion on his face. Kou follows his gaze and instantly stiffens knowing what she did. Forcing a laugh she tries to come up with something. "We a little disagreement last night. Nothing a good sleep on the couch can't fix, if you know what I mean."

Shaking his head slightly to refocus he gives Kou their schedule. It was then, in the corner of her eye, Kou saw Leo moving. As he was bringing himself to his feet she went straight into undercover mode.

"Morning! Did you have enough time to think last night?" She smiled to herself. Maybe this would be fun after all.

It took Leo a moment to process what she was doing. "Ah. Yeah. I'm sorry. You were right. We good?"

The look on the face of the man was clear that he wasn't sure what to think. "You two are the ones we heard about? The new head computer tech and doctor? I heard a lot of strings were pulled to make this happen. An opportunity like this doesn't come along often and I honestly didn't expect you two to be so young. I hope you know how fortunate you both are. Don't mess up this opportunity."

"We humbly apologize. Being here is an honor, sir." Kou looks at Leo to agree.

"Every couple has their bumps," Leo tells him, never looking away from Kou. "I promise it won't happen again."

Leo was staring into a pair of devious eyes he hadn't known before. "We good?" he asks Kou. With on hand on the door he slides the other arm around her waist, pulling her closer.

"Yeah. We're good."

"Good." Leo shuts the door slow enough to give the man standing outside their door a teasing show.

Once the door was closed their lips were only inches apart. Leo, still half asleep expresses, "I hate you," in a exhausted sigh. "I can't believe you started our first fight without me."

"Mmm. I hate you too," Kou said in the same manner.

That morning they were put in a conference room where they would meet with the President himself. The silence of the wait made them so anxious that when the door finally opened they jumped.

"I didn't mean to scare you kids." Mr. President smiles generously.

Leo and Kou grounded themselves and stood up to greet him. Leo reaching out to shake his hand. "It's honor Mr. President."

"The honor is all mine!" He gestures for them to take their seat. As they did he took the corer chair. "I've heard great things about you two. One being you both went to some of the best collages. You must be some smart young adults. I couldn't say no to take Leo on! Then, curiously, I get a strong request if I take Leo I must include Kou, too." He shakes his head smiling. "Now I understand. Young love, right? Who am I to separate a couple soon to married! It really takes me back. I meet my love about your age too. Though, I would have to say I've never quite received such a request as this before. You two must be really something special. In your professions as well as together. I really can't wait to see what you two have in store for us."

"Thank you, Mr. President," Leo pays his respect.

"So, you two are really together, right?" Mr. President asks after a pause.

"Yes, we are," Leo tells him as factual as he could.

Mr. President shake his head. "I'm not convinced. I'm hearing this. I'm seeing you together, but to be honest, I don't feel it."

That statement had Leo squirming in his seat. What gave them away? He opened his mouth but nothing came out.

Thankfully Kou cut in and responds, "we get that a lot. To be completely honest with you, as much as we care for each other, we have dedicated ourselves to our jobs first. We respect the need for professionalism and we are trying to make a good impression for you. We wouldn't want to be seen as careless about our responsibilities just because we have the privilege to work here together. Because we are so dedicated to what we do is why we wanted a job in the same place. We could never continue our relationship otherwise. We want to make both work, but as you can see were still figuring out how to balance."

The present nods absorbing that information. "You two are indeed smart kids. I have gut feeling about these things. And my gut is telling me that you both are going learn a lot more by being here." He leans back in the chair. "I see you two are very scholastic but you need more people skills. Therefore, I want you to invite you to my party this evening. I'm holding a private ball. It will help you put those people skills into action. That way, you can also feel more at ease with being yourselves here before you start your work tomorrow. I respect your professionalism, though."

"Thank you, Mr. President. We won't let you down." Leo smiles broadly.

The President stands up to shake Leo's hand. "I count on it. Welcome to the family," he said before leaving the room.

As the time for the ball crept closer they had been sent a verity of clothing to choose from. Their first mission was to pick out dressy attire!

Kou came out in a long silk green dress. "I think we should practice." Neither of them had danced before. There was no time for such recreation at the alliance.

"That's nice." Leo looks at down at her dress. "I mean aside from the black we have to wear everyday." He smiles at her before approaching closer. "From what I've seen I think this is how it goes."

One hand slipping around her waist and a hand in hers they look down at their feet. Pressing on her mid back Leo moves them. Taking cautious steps for testing.

Kou was astonished he did as well as he did. With his confidant attitude and his role as lead, perhaps they could do this after all.

"As long as they don't demand any fancy dances I think we've got this down," Leo tells her.

"I agree." Kou drops her hand from him. There was no need to keep going if there was nothing more to work on. Their unusual closeness made her feel awkward for some reason. She couldn't tell if he felt the same or not.

When the time came for the dance they entered the ballroom linked arm in arm. A few of the guests greeted them, but as soon as the music started they all took their positions on the floor.

Remembering what they had practiced they moved together with ease. The song was simple and they were able to move about however they wanted.

"Hey. Keep your eyes up here. Up at me," Leo coaxed.

"Right. Sorry."

"I get you have to look at his face, but as of this moment it's the face you love, so act like it!"

They laugh together quietly at the inside joke. But Kou soon realized their laugh between them was real! It was the first real thing they did together being here. It made her all the more shy. She had to fight the urge to look away.

Keeping their mission in mind she looked up courageously. Right into the eyes of Leo Crawford, her fiancé. In his act he seemed rather stuck up on himself, but seeing his eyes up close she almost thought she saw something else hidden in them.

Who really was Leo right now? Was she looking at the Leo she knew from the alliance or her pretend fiancé? But the Leo she was dancing with, right now, was someone she didn't recognize. Could it be? No! She wouldn't think like that. The last thing she needed was to get emotionally caught up in their pretend. That's all they were. Pretend.

Leo sighs. "Apart of me wishes we could just stay in our mission."

Kou tilts her head at him. Wait. What did he mean by that? She watches him as he observes his surroundings. It was silly of her to get her hopes up on that statement, but apart of her understood it too. "I get it. This life is full of pleasures. Everything you could ever need and want is right at your fingertips. Even if it meant keeping you as my pretend fiancé, I really could live my life here. It's almost as if we could forget everything that is really happening outside. I already have to remind myself none of this is real. That none of it could be." She found herself looking down again. Wondering if she said too much. She hadn't meant to.

"Unfortunately, at some point, it will have to end," he sympathizes.

As the night went on they danced alongside the other couples. Even the President and his wife were dancing and having a good time.

Leo subtly observed it all. It was interesting to know what things took place behind the scenes in The White House. And he knew there was still so much yet to discover.

The dance was soon to be over, but Kou was starting to limp. On noticing Leo caught her, steadying her back up.

"I've never worn heels before," Kou admitted. "They're starting to take their toll."

Pushing on the smaller part on her back, Leo applied enough pressure for her to lean on him more. "Here. I've got your though the rest of this song. I think this may be the last."

She hesitated a moment before complying. On doing so it brought ease to her aching feet, but it also brought them closer. A lot closer.

"Thanks," she whispers under her breath.

Leo was right. It was the last song of the night and soon after everyone said their goodbyes to leave. Making it just outside the ballroom door themselves Kou takes a hold of Leo's arm so she could pull off her heels.

"Should I carry you, love?" he says teasingly.

"You'll do no such thing!" she spits at him.

He flings his arms back submissively.

Immediately taking up her clothes to go change she voiced over shoulder that she could take the couch tonight. "You had it last night. It's only fair." Not hearing him decline she assumes he agreed with her.

Coming back out of the bathroom she saw sound asleep in the bed. Leaving her with a blanket and pillow for the couch.

Covering herself up the couch she soon realized it was a very comfortable sitting couch, but the longer she laid there the more she ached. After tossing and turning she sits up to plop back down. Ugh! "How did Leo sleep like this last night? Was he really this uncomfortable?"

"Can't sleep?"

"You're awake? Were you awake last night too?"

"Something like that," he mumbles.

"Why didn't you say anything?" She sits upright. How was she going to do this? Her gaze fell down to the floor wondering if that would be more comfortable.

"And what? Expect you to let me sleep with you?" Leo replies.

"I don't know. Maybe?"

Leo moves over to one side of the bed. "Come on already. Big day tomorrow."

It didn't take too much convincing. They did have a big first day working tomorrow. They had to be rested and at their best. There wasn't much time to make one another comfortable. After all they're engaged. That meant day and night.

"Fine." She shuffles her way over and climbs in the bed.

Chapter Ten

Walking into a room full of computers Leo saw the line up of screens on a the wall as well. It was a different set up then what he was used to, but nothing he couldn't handle.

"Sir." One of the men spoke.

Leo scans his badge. "Johnson?"

"Yes, Sir." Johnson straightens up.

"My name is Leo Crawford. Unlike your previous boss I do not have a Navy or Military background. Therefore, I feel no need for you to address me as such. You may address me as Boss, Crawford, or Sir. I trust we can work together and accomplish our tasks accordingly. Unless you need such order?"

"No, Sir!" The words came out instinctively from them.

Leo imagined himself shaking his head. Such formality wasn't something he was accustomed to, but he would have to get used to it. "As you were." He nods to them to disperse.

As they did so he sat at the computer off to the side. The previous head left him papers of everything he needed to know and what they were currently doing. He flips through them to figure out where he should start. He took advantage of being new to check everything out he could. That way anyone else would assume he was getting accustomed to things without suspicion of an alter addenda.

In another area of the White House Kou found her way to Doctor Iris, who had been waiting for her.

Iris showed her where she could find what she needed in any given situation.

Kou had never worked in an actual hospital before, so she was grateful for all the extra schooling she was able to get with Astra's help. This would be incredible opportunity to test her knowledge and grow more in her skills without the use of her gift.

While doing her best to keep up with everything, Kou's mind began to wander to the possible future outcomes of being in The White House. One, making her stop walking altogether. They didn't know how long they would be there for. If it happened to be for some time, would she and Leo have to start planning for a wedding?

"We have some guards who are waiting for a little patch work. Are you up for that Docter Kawa?"

"Yes, I am." Kou quickly regains her focus.

Doctor Iris brought in the few men dressed as guards. They clearly had scrapes, burns, and cuts.

"May I ask what happened?" Docter Iris questions.

"We had rioters around The White House trying to get in again. There's this particular group that were getting physical. I don't think they really mean to do any harm, but it could come to that."

"I see."

Kou was more confused than satisfied with that answer. Why would they be doing that?

The cut on the one guard was deep, but thankfully there was no dire need for her to use her gifts at this point. She took what they had to stitch him up. While she did so she wondered how Leo was doing...

Leo studied all the papers on his desk. Assessing everything he could do under his title. It was a lot to remember, but with one finger on those keys he could do whatever he wanted.

Setting all the papers aside his hands went to the keyboard to start playing around with what he could get into. Trying it all out. He currently started tinkering with the security monitors. He was able to see what everyone else was doing in The White House at any given time. He could see it all!

Click. Click. Click. He stumbled onto the camera for the Hospital ward and noticed Kou. He watches her as she dismiss a patient and brings in another. He zooms in slightly. Enough to confirm what he thought he saw. Yes, it was! Kou was smiling! She was genuinely enjoying what she was doing.

He leans back on his chair thinking what she said the other night at the ball. She was right. This was all like a dream they could easily get sucked into. He too had to remember none of it was real.

Tinkering with the security cameras again he found a weapons room. Must be a precaution in case of a threat on The White House. While observing the weapons he saw, in the upper right hand corner, a light blinking. What did that mean again?

He moves his mouse to click on it, but what he found was something he couldn't begin to fathom. It was the reason why they were here. He knew things were bad in the barrier but he didn't how bad. "Oh."

The day was nearly done and Kou was thanking Doctor Iris for all her help when a red light above their heads started spinning. The sound deafening.

Kou covers her ears, "what is that?"

"Not again!" Iris rushes around to calls in the surgical team. "We need to prep for immediate surgeries. Can you help?"

Kou nods and starts prepping for whatever may come through the doors. She took one deep breath to focus as the doors were slammed open.

A guard was carried in and Doctor Iris took the lead of assessing this one herself. "You get the next one!" Docter Iris tells Kou on passing.

When the doors open again Kou rushes to the aid of the woman. Without any hesitation she gets the woman to the surgical room. She didn't much time to register that the woman was the President's wife.

Kou hovers around her assessing her injures. Instinctively, Kou scans her body with her gift. What else could she do? A dark smoky color, along with blood, covered her face and body.

"What happened out there!" Kou shouted to the ones who had brought her in. "I need to know what's happening so I can help her!"

"An explosion," one of the men spoke up.

Her patient, laying on her table, was barely conscious. Kou already knew the only way to save her life would be to use her gift. Using her eyes she found an inner bleed. "We need to do this now!"

This wasn't what she thought her first day on job was going to be like. She was handed her implement and she made the incision. Only to visually see how much worse the injury was.

Kou knew her odds of survival were minimal, so she did what she had to do, but made sure to do it subtly. Using her tool alongside her gift. If anyone noticed they didn't say anything. It was risky, but it was worth it.

"Doctor," one of helpers with her interrupted her concentration. "Does she have a chance?"

"I-"

Beeeee.

Kou's head rose at the sound, looking at the monitor before working to correct any problems. She couldn't lose her! She wouldn't! She closes her eyes a moment to reach out. Trying to see if her body would take anything in her weakened state, but the sound only kept going.

"Time of death," Kou spoke quietly.

Silent eyes stared at her. Everyone in shock at how fast they lost her. When, "Doctor Kawa!" one spoke.

Looking back at the monitor she saw a heart beat! Her body was fighting again! It had worked! After that surgery continued to go smoothly for them.

Soon the door to the surgical opened. "Doctor Kawa. Doctor Iris needs your assistance."

Kou nods. She would have to be more careful around Doctor Iris. She would be watching her closely. Now that she understood what was going on perhaps she wouldn't need to use her gifts. Regardless of how would proceed she was going to do her best to save the guard.

Scrubbing in to help Doctor Iris she realizes that she recognizes this guard. He was the one on duty the night they arrived!

Getting to work she goes over everything in her mind before making any decisions. All she could do was her best and so far it was working. Of course, like it was with the First Lady, things changed fast.

"We're losing him!"

Kou and Doctor Iris's hands speed up. With Kou's heart beating just as fast she felt her whole body aching to take her control to help him. She could try to heal him, but if she did there would be questions she could not answer. Even with good intentions she could very well be putting herself and Leo in danger by using her gifts. She couldn't blow their cover. The mission had to take priority. Yet, as a Doctor, she couldn't let her patient die either!

"Doctor Kawa! What did you do here?"

Using her insight to see Kou tries something quickly, but they were running out of time, "it's not working!"

Doctor Iris steps up, following her lead. "I have any idea! He still might have a chance."

All at once things were put into place and all was quiet. They stopped. Watching. Waiting. Nothing. With held breaths released Kou drops her head. Eye lashes fluttering as she processes everything that had happened. When-

Beeeee.

"There's nothing wrong!" Kou shouts. "What's happening?"

"His body is done fighting," Docter Iris told her. "There's nothing more we can do. Kou, I'm not gong to tell you this is something you get used to. You don't. But I am proud of what you were able to do today. I don't know how you did it but you saved the First Lady. For that you will be heavily rewarded."

Kou listens but doesn't respond. When she knew they were done she pushed her way out. She couldn't change and get back to her room fast enough. It may not have been her fault but she hadn't lost a patient before.

Leo was sitting on the couch with his laptop in hand, fingers typing when she came in. He hadn't known what happened exactly, but the look on her face said enough. Uncrossing his legs he sat the laptop on the cushion next to him and stood up.

Tears fell from her eyes the moment she squeezed them shut. She couldn't move, couldn't see, couldn't speak. Sorrow had a hold on her heart and it wasn't letting her go.

Fallen into complete darkness behind her eyelids she felt a warm touch. They wrapped her up, allowing her head to rest. The gentle gesture broke her from withdrawing into herself and allowed the verbal sounds of distress to accompany her cries. "I couldn't save him! I couldn't use my gifts to save him!"

Leo strokes her head. This day was challenging for both of them, but he couldn't imagine how much more it was for Kou. This mission

they took on was far from anything they could have prepared for. One thing was all too clear. All they had was each other.

Chapter Eleven

After a month at The White House it came time to check in with Astra. To do so Leo and Kou had went for a walk in the gardens.

With his mouth close to the watch Leo spoke, "as far as we can tell no one is suspicious about what were planning. And it doesn't look like there are any Rouge Spies lingering about. We're currently in the clear, but from my findings I suggest that we implement Vicki soon. Things are only getting worse. If this doesn't succeed I have no doubt everyone inside this artificial life will become extinct. By anything but gradually."

"You're right," Astra's voice spoke back to him. "Tomorrow makes a new month. Come up with a plan to leave and get yourself to the meeting point tomorrow. I'll give you more details at that point. It's time to proceed with Vicki."

"Understood."

"Astra out."

Leo sighs as he turns to Kou. "This is it."

Nodding, Kou slips her palm into his offered hand so they could weave their way back through the garden. Their pretending had become more natural. Of course, their friendship had grown stronger than what it had been too. It was nice, for both of them, to be so well understood.

Entering The White House they walked the empty hallways. At this time of the evening most were settling in for the night. Only one lone shadow grew on the carpet before them. Knowing that Leo stops them.

It confused Kou, who was lost in thought about what they had to do for tomorrow. Looking up at it him something about it felt different. It felt real. Had he gotten that good at pretending?

Now facing each other Kou's eyes sparkled up at Leo as he reached out to run his fingers through her hair. No doubt they both had excelled at their acting skills to stay in character. But even Leo often thought, if he didn't know better, she could have had him easily fooled too.

"Oh, there you two are!" a voice calls to them. "I've been keeping my eye out for you two all day," the President said. "I must say it's been so nice to have you here. You've both exceeded my expectations by far!"

"Thank you," Kou spoke warmly. "You've been so kind to us. We will always be grateful for this opportunity."

"I think I'm one who should be thanking you, Kou. If it weren't for you my wife would not be here today."

Kou's cheeks turn rosy. She nods but didn't say anything more on the subject.

"Well," the President continues, "I hope, as your first month here draws to a close, that you'll have many more wonderful opportunities to keep you interested in. I haven't a head tech quite like Leo before, either! We need more young people like the both of you. So, promise me after you set a date for your wedding that you will come back!"

"Thank you, Mr. President," Leo acknowledges respectfully.

"Okay! Well, that's about it! You kids have a good night." The president straightens his shirt before walking off.

Thinking about how long they'd been there, how far they've come in their expanding their skills, and grown as individuals they knew they fell into the trap of becoming too comfortable. Neither of them said a word on their way back to their room.

Once back Kou climbs into the bed. "Tell me what you see in the computer room," Kou asks facing Leo.

Leo swung his head to this side, looking at her. "What?"

"I know you don't like to talk about it. What's going out there. I'm afraid that I may be too caught up this fantasy to want to leave. I'd like to refocus on the mission. Even if I don't want this to end, I know it must. One way or another it will. That's why I need you to tell me what's really happening."

Leo shifts, facing her. "That first day I came across these channels that were tuned in from all around the word. There were too many to flip through them all. What I saw were wars, sickness, pollution, and so much more I can't explain. It's all due to the barrier. Our world is dying."

"Not if we can help it."

"I know this life would be nice to live out but it's an illusion. Everything inside the barrier is." Leo looks down, thinking. "That being said, I wish we didn't have to leave either."

Kou giggles softly, "even if it meant having to be my pretend fiancé forever? So," Kou refocuses, "what do we tell them tomorrow so we can leave?"

As Kou was talking Leo mumbled something, but she hadn't caught it in time to understand. "What was that?" she asks.

"Try taking out the pretend."

"Taking out the...?" A creased line on her forehead relaxes at the realization of what he had said. "What are you saying?"

"We've had our whole lives focused on something greater than this world we know, so it wasn't something I took time to think about before. A lot of people have put aside things to help our future, but I'm not sure if I want to explore that new future without you. You may not feel like that and that's okay. As long as we remain close friends."

Unsure what to say Kou stared at him. How long had he felt that way? When did all this pretending change into something real? And did she, in return, really feel the same?

This mission already caused some confusing and conflicting emotions. But one thing was for sure. He was there for her when she needed it, and she had to admit that Leo was one of the most caring people she knew. Actions don't lie. There was, no doubt, proof of something real in their pretending.

She felt a smile tugging at her lips. Oh, how awkward they were when they started this mission! Whether it was their first pretend hug, kiss, fight, or dance. Though, it was just an act, she cherished those memories.

Leo's brows came together seeing her expression. "What?"

"I was thinking about all the things we did. Our first dance! Our first fight. All of those pretend things. All those pretend kisses." She pauses, eyes darting away. "How many kisses did it take before we got the one that became real?" When she was brave enough to look up she saw an expression that was completely perplexed.

Leo moved his head away contemplating. When did *this* between them happen? He couldn't say. It crept up on them so silently until it grew too loud to ignore. He sat up but then stopped, "can I touch you? Once I do, it won't be pretend anymore."

Kou nods. Waiting to feel the warmth of his outstretched hand moving toward her face. He never asked permission when they were pretending. There were still so many firsts ahead of them. Including the fluttering feeling in her stomach that told her this was very real. Smiling, she reaches out for his face too.

"What do we say tomorrow to get away?" Kou asks. They still needed a good plan.

"We'll say that we had an energy phone call in the night and that we need to leave because one of our grandmother's is dying. And at this time we're not sure when we will be back."

"Sad. That sounds reasonable, though. He would let us do that."

"Good. Then we'll send him a message first thing and get ready to go."

"The most challenging gig yet!" Kou squints her eyes at him.

"In the mean time let's not worry about tomorrow until tomorrow comes."

"Deal."

"Good. Come here," he orders.

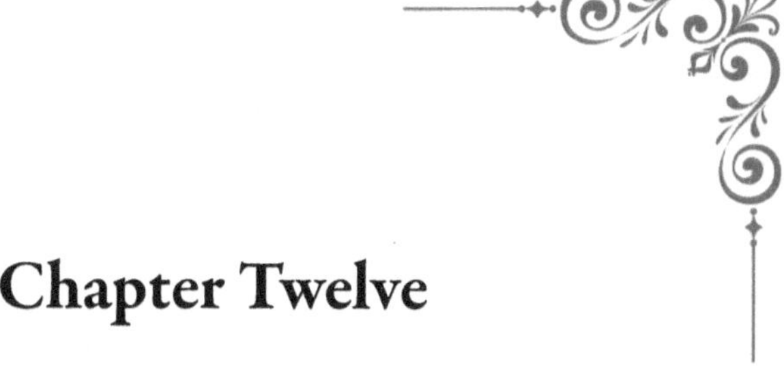

Chapter Twelve

In the morning they sent their note off with a messenger right as they finished packing. They hadn't talked to the President himself about their leave, but they knew he trusted them. If they didn't run into him on the way out they hoped he would understand one day.

"I wonder how everyone is doing." Kou's mind wanders to her friends in the alliance as she zips up her last bag. "I hope everyone is safe."

Leo sets his ready bag next to hers. "They are."

"I really like Riona. Odd girl," Kou smiles to herself, "but such a kind heart. I hope she's doing okay too."

"She's with Riv. I'm sure they're doing just fine. As long as they haven't turned on one another! Now that, I would pay to see."

Kou eyes widen. "They would never!" She could his point, though. Riv found his match. It would be quite entertaining to see them fight, considering their strong personalities.

"Let's go." Leo takes their bags in one hand and Kou's hand in the other. They left the door open behind them and made their way to the elevator.

Watching the numbers dropping on panel in front of them Leo noticed something off. A kind of electric in blue followed down the veins in his hand. That wasn't something that often happened, but when it did a high energy source was near. The first time it happened was when the Rogue Droids were near.

Adjusting himself, he tries to stay in tune with the source. Reaching out to touch the panel another wave of light rushes down his arm. The electric burst left his fingers and went straight to the panel, stopping the elevator. He stumbles backward at the sudden jolt of energy. His gift of electrical sensing had never left his body like that before.

"Did you know you could do that?"

"No. I don't think it's the elevator panel that has my senses on edge. Something's coming."

"Leo. You stopped the elevator. Can you start it again?"

His gaze drops to his hands. Good question. Could he? He had always tinkered with computers and got what he wanted. This couldn't be much different, right? It's all just power.

As his fingers moved to feel it out energy revved up in him. Directing another zap outward to the panel. The stopped elevator jumped slightly before moving again.

"Are your gifts growing stronger?"

Leo said nothing. That was a possibility, but his senses told him otherwise.

Stopping at the first floor a blast of air threw them back as the door cracked opened. Finding themselves on the floor they crawled to peek out. It was dusky and dark, but the hallway was clearly collapsed. The only light in the haze was the light illuminating from Leo.

"The White House is under attack." That's what he was feeling! Something on the outside was powerful enough for him to sense. "And more is about to come."

"The Rouges?" Kou lifts herself to her feet.

"No, the Rogues have no idea we're here. But what I've been seeing, like I told you, it's only a matter of time before everything and everyone hits their breaking point. This cage the Rouges put us in is taking its toll. We can't take the pressure of being contained forever. These people don't know why they're acting like this and it's not entirely their fault. If we can't get out to implement Vicki this world as we know it will come to an end. Then the Rouges will truly have all the power in the world."

"Then we need to find away to get out of here."

Leo closes his eyes trying to reach out to any power source still running. Much was down but he kept trying to feel what he could use around him. He hadn't used his gift to this extent before, but they needed to get out before another attack came. That he could feel. They didn't have much time.

"I think I have something."

The flickering of light ran down his hand to the tips of his fingers. At the same time any remaining overhead lights in the hallway burnt out and shattered. It was enough power to open the door another inch. Leo pushed at it but it didn't budge any further.

"There's no way to get it to open anymore. As strange as it sound I may be able to to fry it. Which may open it. Like a shock and a reflex."

"Will that really work?"

"No, but I have to try."

"Okay." Kou nods. "I trust you."

Electricity, that mimicked the form of lighting, traveled over both of Leo's arms down to his hands. Extending them quickly he throws it to the panel. Turning it black. A moment later the doors screeched. Opening a few inches more. "That should be enough for us to squeeze through!"

Maneuvering their body though the elevator door they tread the halls carefully, avoiding any hazards from the blast.

"I can't believe someone was able to bomb The White House," Kou whispers. "Shouldn't there be people crawling all over the place already?"

"It's likely that their first priority is to put the President in the safe room for the time being. Until they can assess the situation. Which I'm sure won't be long, though. We best get out of here before we get caught in the middle."

Reaching the front doors they climb over fallen beams and broken glass hand in hand. Until they finally make their way out.

"So much for our a peaceful life," Leo reminisces.

"When I asked for a reality check I didn't know it would be so extreme."

"Shh," Leo put his finger to his lips. They were outside, but there was no sound whatsoever. Looking around there was no one in sight either. Tightening his grip on her hand they ran.

They kept running as far and long as their legs could take them. Finally understanding why they were all trained to run back at the warehouse. It may have well saved their life.

"Will everyone we left at The White House be okay?" Kou breaths in.

"Only if what we do succeeds."

There was nothing more they could do but to finish their mission. They would have to be willing to try or life as they knew it would come to an end.

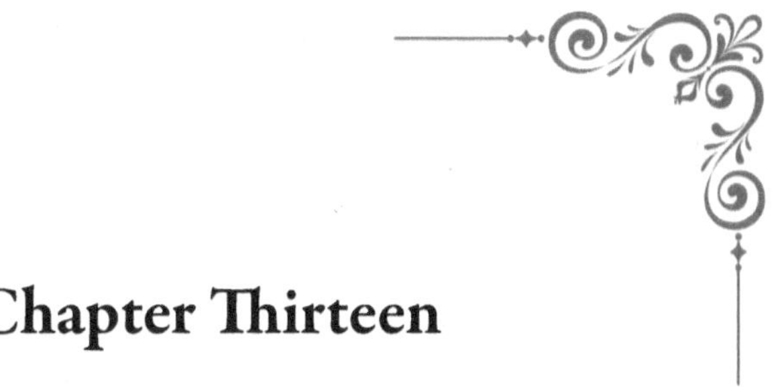

Chapter Thirteen

Da ding ding. Da ding ding.

"River. What is it?"

River and Riona were sitting around the camp fire with his father, sister, and other family when the watch he wore to communicate with Astra went off. Riona knew the tone when Astra would call, but she never heard this one.

River looks up at everyone before speaking, "it's time."

Riona, holing Memengwaa's baby, stood up to hand her over to her grandfather.

"Astra sent the message to every alliance, "River tells them. "Leo and Kou are with Astra as well." River looks at Riona, who was melting in her seat with relief. "They're not far from the stream that connects here. That's where they're going to implement the virus."

"Then get ready my children," Niigaanii tells them.

River rushes to his feet to start gathering their belongings while Riona went with Memengwaa.

Memengwaa was retuning Riona's clothes. Riona stares down at them as it was handed to her. It was her clothes given to her by the alliance.

"I patched them up for you," Memengwaa said. "These will do you more good on your journey than what you have on now."

Riona gives her thanks. Despite the memories last connected with wearing those clothes Memengwaa was right. She couldn't fight this battle in her current attire.

Meeting up with River they both stoped, seeing each other. They both looked like they had before in alliance with Astra. So much had happened between then and now. But now, they were more evolved than they once were.

Helping Riona into the canoe River soon follows. Looking up they saw his family there to see them off.

"We will give you the head start," Niigaanii told them. "My son, "he points to his son in law who was getting into the water, "will guide you as far as he is able to save time off your journey. We will prepare here. We won't be far behind."

"Thank you, father."

"There's nothing a father wouldn't do for his son." Niigaanii then looks at Riona. "Or daughter."

On reaching the deeper part of the water Adrian tells them to hold on before swimming under. Pointing them in the right direction Adrian gives them a big push that would cut their travel time in half. Coming back to the surface Adrian waves them off.

Now that they were on their own they took up rowing to keep the canoe going straight until they reached the other side. Not far in the distance she could see those from the alliance gathering.

Stepping out onto the grass Riona hears her name being called out.

"Riona!"Kou was running toward her until they were embraced in each other arms.

Riona hadn't realized how much she had missed her. Squeezing her tight before letting go she looks up to Leo walking toward her to. Leo opens his arms wide, ready to embrace her.

"It's hard not to worry about our friends." Leo engulfs her.

She giggles. "I missed you too, Leo."

River, now walking to her side after pulling the canoe up, heard the last of what was spoken.

"Hm," Leo clears his throat. "It's good to see you both safe."

Riona sucks in her lips as she gave Kou a look. Leo and Kou looked so happy. She didn't need her gifts to tell her why. It was easy to see.

Being front and center Astra was breaking everyone into groups. Most of them would be watchmen and guardians if anything came in too close to camp.

"Riv!" Astra shouts out. "You are watchmen and guardian inside the camp! You will be watching the workers backs. Leo! You're lead of Vicki. You're front and center. No pressure! Kou! Floater! If anyone needs assistance you know what to do. Riona! You got Leo's and Kou's six!"

Riona breaths in at the sound of those words. She had her assignment and yet she felt like Astra could have made better use of her. Was she trying to keep her safe? She was glad to work alongside her friends, but she couldn't help but wonder if her assignment had anything to do with River's previous concerns.

A touch on her arm cleared her wandering thoughts. River had laid his hand on her. With one shared look any thought that was his was now hers. She understood. "It's okay. I got this. I promise." Whatever assignment she had, it was important, and she would do her best.

After everyone received their assignments and were dismissed she turned into River, who held her tightly. Everything they did led up to this moment in time. They both had to believe they were ready. No matter what might happen. Knowing she could never physically hurt him she gave him the tightest embrace she could manage before reluctantly letting go. Kou and Leo would be waiting for her.

Hand in hand, Riona led River with her to find Kou setting up Leo's workstation near the field while Leo was throwing stones at it. The field buzzed at this next toss. Shimmering so briefly that anyone could have missed it if they didn't know what they were looking at.

"How long until they know were here?" River asks.

"As soon as I put the drive in they'll know somethings up. It won't take them long to track us after that. And depending on where they have scouts or Rouge Droids it could be anywhere from half hour to a few hours for them to engage us, if that's what they decide to do."

"When do we do this?" Riona asks.

"How 'bout first thing tomorrow?" Astra's voice resonates from behind her.

Spinning on her heels Riona smiles. "Hi, aunt Astra."

Riona saw her roll her eyes but something told her she was relieved to see her, too.

"Aunt Astra, what if we get caught by anyone other than the Rouges? How do we know we're safe from interruption from either side?"

"As of right now the government has no idea. We made sure of that properly when picking out this particular location. But that's what the watchmen are for. Anyone would have to go through them before discovering us here and by then we would know."

"Makes sense," Rioan nods.

"I suggest that all you young ones get a good night's rest. No parties. We haven't won yet." Astra gave a stern look as she walks away. "We will have plenty enough time to celebrate when we do win."

"Awe. But I love parties," Leo voice trails off. Sounding as disappointed at he could.

The girls laugh but River, standing next Riona, stood strong. With his arms crossed and a look anyone else could only guess. When Leo caught sight of it he stiffens his stance slightly.

Riona reaches out to link arms Kou. "There's so much I wish I could tell you."

"Me too."

Chapter fourteen

Sunrise crept over the hills as all in the alliance woke. Tents were put away and the work for today began. While groups of the guardians and watchmen were heading out in every direction to keep an eye on things Leo took the drive, Vicki, out of his pocket. He simply had to wait for the go ahead.

Riona and River wandered about the camp to watch everything in motion. The guardians were already taking their leave to their posts, but Riona was thankful that River was assigned inside the camp as a guardian and watchmen. They wouldn't be far apart that way.

One group taking off was those of really tall stature. "What are they?" Riona inquires. "They're so tall."

"I don't know their specific name. We've called them the Giants for as long as I've know them. They're very proud of it."

Riona watches the Giants and all the other species around her. All holding their special gifts. They all come together to take back what was rightfully theirs. Her eyes smiles. Only the faintest recollection of it was on her lips.

"How's it coming Leo?" Astra approaches to check on their progress.

"Everything is up and running. All I need to do it put the drive in into the laptop and start fighting the digital fight with this invisible field."

"Are we ready to begin?" River asks Astra from behind.

Taking a deep breath she nods. "We're as ready as we can be."

Leo looks at them silently as he reaches down to take a hold of Vicki. He nods before he pushes it into the laptop. It chirped. Putting his fingers on the keyboard Leo braces for action. "Here we go," he said under his breath.

"All alert!" Astra's voice rang out. "Our fight has begun! Let's win this thing once and for all!"

The morning crept by far too quiet for their liking. They expected the worse and a lot more action. Either way Leo kept taping on the keyboard trying to open the border.

Ba-ding.

"What was that?" Kou peers over Leo's shoulder.

"I'm in!" Leo throws his hands up. "I can take control! It'll take me a minute." Leo smiles up briefly before getting back to work. "Vicki is working."

Riona reaches out to River feeling the ease in the tense atmosphere. A lot of people were counting on them. That in itself was a lot of pressure to hold.

"It's not over yet," River speaks up. "It's never that easy. Be prepared for anything."

Leo nods. "Acknowledged."

Hmmmmmm. Hmmmmmm.

Leo, Kou, River, Riona, and Astra look at each other. They were listening to a sound they hadn't heard before. It was far outside the camp but it was getting louder every second.

Suddenly nervous Riona froze. "What is that?"

River walks a few steps out. Sensing, he closes his eyes. When he turns back to look at them he draws out his escrima stick. "They're Rouge Droids. Hundreds of them."

"Leo! Keep working," Astra orders as she joins Riv. Also pulling out her escrima stick from behind her. "Just in case any slip by our guardians we'll be ready."

Riona took Kou's hand. Assuring her. She was Kou and Leo's last defense. And she would protect them at all costs. As Astra and River went off to watch the perimeter Riona kept close to Leo Kou.

Their camp was elevated so they were able to see downward. Overlooking the trees they could see a grey haze starting to raise over the top of them. The guardians were doing their job to destroy the Rouge Droids and as a result the entire woods became swallowed by smoke. It was only a matter of time until the Rouge Droids adapted, too. They always did.

"Hey!" Astra yells over she shoulder. "Where are we with the field?"

Leo, typing as fast as he could responds, "field is down 62%. I need more time!"

De-de. De-de. The watch around Astra wrist lit up. Holding it close she presses a button.

"They're adapting! They're on their way to you! Repeat! They're heading to you!" a distressed voice from one of the guardians warns.

Stretching her neck Astra steps forward, preparing her stance. "Here we go."

Past the thickened atmosphere the Rouge Droids were fighting their way through by rising higher into the sky. Flying over the trees and straight for the border.

"If you could get that field down within 15 minutes that would great Leo!" Astra yells out.

"I'm almost there!" Leo taps faster and rhythmically. Right in front of him the invisible field flashed. It was now fluctuating in its strength. "45%!"

Riona stood her ground trying to be ready for whatever came. She could do this! She wasn't without her gifts. Knowing she could maneuver objects she could most likely, she thought, move the Rouge Droids out of the aim of fire. If needed, she slips a hand in her pocket, she had her knife.

Bzzz.

One Rouge Droid came at them low, taking them by surprise, but they were ready! Astra struck at it, taking it out. That was just the start of them sneaking in.

Riona shifted her weight on her heels. Waiting for the time where she would need to take action as well. That time would come far too soon.

HMMM.

The sound was deafening. A swarm of Rouge Droids were coming at them. Flying high above them. Pew! Pew! A few of the Rouge Droids were coming in too close for comfort. Ducking, Astra sends them away with a forceful swat. One of the Rouge Droids now spinning over to River, who had plenty of his share to take care off.

"Knife!"

Riona looks at River. Knife? Oh! Without another thought she threw it at him. He caught it in time to throw it at a Rouge Droid just out of reach.

"Riona! Over there." Kou warns about one sneaking away from the main fight.

"Got it." Positioning herself on the other side of Leo she waited for its arrival. She could handle a few fine. When the time came she drew her elbows back before outstretching them. Pushing them, the few Rouge Droids collided into one another and exploded.

The sound captures Astra and River's attention. Turning around with concern they see what had happened. Their faces then becoming satisfied.

"I taught her everything she knows." River grins to Astra.

"You don't say!" Astra cocks her head at him. "Good work my niece! Oh, hang on. A group of them is coming."

Astra was right. Their hum was like that of a hive of bees moving together. With so many the ground under their feet started to rattle.

"Leo, don't look back." Riona steps up, ready to defend her friends.

The heat of the fight became quite intense. It was now a full out war between the Rouge Droids and them. And many of the guardians made their way back up to help better assist them inside the camp.

Riona, having her hands full, took down a Rouge Droid that slipped past the others. Her strategy, pushing and colliding, was working so she kept at. Perfecting that pattern of fighting as they came. Until she was exploding multiple together at a time.

Knowing that it was only a matter of time before they adapted to her technique, she knew she needed to figure out her next plan of action. Perhaps she could spin them around herself to throw them off enough to keep doing what she was. It was her only move but it was working! As long as it kept Leo and Kou safe.

But they were already adapting. It was getting harder to move them about like she had been. Riona groaned. They were spreading too far apart. She would have to push them away for the time being.

Finding her strength she positions herself between them. Letting them circle her. Reaching for the furthest Rouge Droids she launches them forward to hit all the others in the process. Ducking at the collision.

Pew! Pew! The lesser damaged kept firing.

"They keep adapting!" Riona yells over her shoulder. "Do you have it?"

"One more minute! One more minute!" Leo sweats.

Riona did everything in her power to keep the heat off Leo. The fire became heavy. Almost too heavy to handle alone. She dropped to the grass, missing a shot that ended up hitting Leo's laptop. The sound of it crashing was unmistakable.

"No, no, no, no!" Leo threw his hands over his head. "I AMLOST HAD IT! ROUGES! ROUGES!"

They had all fought too hard to lose. Gritting her teeth Riona ran at the Rouge Droids in frustration. Using all the strength she had in her to fight them. Somehow, almost instinctively, she pushes her hands downwards to lift herself into the air.

Being closer to the Rouge Droids she was able to move them around with ease. Manipulating them and crashing them down to the earth. They hadn't adapted to it yet so she kept at it. It was as if her rage was keeping her going. But rage alone wasn't going to win this fight.

Something else was fueling her. It was a rare feeling she felt once before when she was training with River at the warehouse. She felt it again now, as the smoke engulfed her from her successful blows, that she didn't notice River watching her in midair.

River, being aware of her anger ran to her. It didn't take long for him to realize what was happening was something he saw in his dreams. The ones he would have nightmares about because it would always follow with her dying. It was coming true.

Stopping mid step something else pulled his thoughts. He had thought he recalled her screaming in his vision before she was killed, but now observing what was in front of him was something new. Something he hadn't seen. It wasn't her death! This was her breakthrough! Her gifts would destroy the Rouge Droids!

"LET GO RIONA! LET GO!" River bellows from the ground. "LET GO!"

Massive groups of Rouge Droids began swarming and hovering around her as she was currently the biggest threat. Yet, through the deafening sound, she had heard him. She understood his meaning.

Closing her eyes, Riona felt it, letting it build up within her. She could do this. For the alliance, for her parents, for her friends, for River. They would not fail if she had anything to do with it.

Her eyes, on opening, were gold. The radiance from her gift clearly showed. Glowing around, not just her eyes, but her entire body. Still afloat her hair then rises from her shoulders. Mouth open, a piercing scream echoes as forceful rush of air disintegrates all the Rouge Droids around her. Causing a cascade of explosions, eliminating most of the Rouge Droids inside the camp.

Leo, paying little attention to what had happned, was in a panic. Kou was trying to assist him the best she could. Thinking of other ways to bring down the barrier, but after seeing Riona's breakthrough it gave Kou an idea.

"Wait. Leo." Kou puts her hands on him.

"I can't believe this!" he repeated.

"Leo!

"What?" He looks at her.

"You are the virus! You. You are the virus. Remember the elevator. You don't need a laptop. We just need you! Think about it! You already have energy inside of you."

"I'm the virus? I- I am the virus!" His eyes light up. "I'm the virus!"

"Yes! Yes!"

Outstretching his hands the barrier begins to sparkle at his incoming touch. The barrier was much more advanced than any computer he had ever worked with. It was a wonder he got as far as he did with Vicki.

Leo laughs. "I have it! It's coming down. Right- now!"

After watching the barrier come down Kou jumped with joy as Leo came to pick her up, spinning her around. "I'm so proud of you! Who would have thought it would be that simple?"

Looking at her dumbfounded, Leo thought about that. "It shouldn't have been."

Pew Pew!

Leo and Kou crouch down. The barrier was down but the attack hadn't stopped. Picking up a near by stick, Kou began swinging it at the Rouge Droids. Striking the two they fall to the ground in a sizzle.

"That's my girl!" Leo praised.

They were on the ground but not completely out of commission. One of Droids wiggles, adjusting it's aim of fire toward Leo. Kou noticed the movement and jumped into action. Raising her stick to finish it. In the mean time the Rouge Droid had already adapted to her methods. Speeding up its fire rate it hits her.

"Guhh."

After Riona took out the majority of the Rouge Droids she floated down to where River was waiting for her. She was immediately swallowed by his embrace the moment her toes touched the ground.

See, "Riona whispered in his ear. "Everything turned out fine."

Tensing, River sensed something wasn't, though. They both turned to see Kou in action to protect Leo and knew what would follow.

Riona took back her pocket knife from River and she ran. As fast as her legs could take her and she threw it at the Droid. As her knife twirled in the air to its destination Riona was hit by the Droid as well. She didn't think twice in taking Kou's place. She already placed herself in front of her. Shielding Kou.

Unfortunately, her knife didn't take the Rouge Droid out. The minor blow put it into a spin while it kept intermittently firing. River had went after it. Avoiding the Droid's unpredictable aims and took it out for good. When he looked up is when he saw Riona in Kou's arms.

With an nauseated feeling rising up in his throat River ran to them. Falling to his knees he hovers. "Kou! Can you heal her?"

Kou held Riona with her free arm as Leo checked her breathing and pulse. Without a word Kou lifts her hand away from her own body to reveal to River a red hand. She, herself, was bleeding out. Except, with help of her inborn gift, her body was trying to heal itself. She wanted to help Riona, but Kou knew she wouldn't be able to do that if she couldn't heal herself. Her injuries were just a life threatening.

Trying to stifle his quivering lips River turns his head away. Riona stopped breathing. He too knew if Kou were to transfer her healing gifts to Riona he would be asking her to take Riona's place. He couldn't ask that. He wouldn't. He shook his head not accepting the one thing he feared.

How selfish it was of him, he thinks. To hope that everything would turn out okay. Many others in the alliance may have lost ones they held dear. He could not be exempt from that fate. Whimpering he turns back to look at Riona. Reaching out to stroke her forehead.

He may have had glazed eyes but he caught Kou shifting herself. Curious what she was doing he watches her place her hand over Riona's wounds. Leaving hers untenanted.

"I can't ask you to do that," River whispers.

"I'm sorry," Leo cuts in, "but I would have to agree."

"Riv. Leo. I don't have enough energy to heal myself. Riona may be gone, but there is a period after death that one could be revived. There's always a chance. We," she chokes, "us both dying will mean nothing if I don't give her that chance."

"No." River shakes his head. There was no guarantee either of them would survive. He gathered Riona up in a hug, supporting her head. Why didn't he foresee this? Why couldn't he see the bigger picture?

Leo aided Kou down. "Are you sure about this?"

Kou nods.

"You wont-. You won't." Leo shakes his head with a pained smile as Kou pulled him down. Forehead to forehead.

With Riona next to her she begins to transfer what healing life source she had to Riona. Kou's now shut eyes moving under her eyelids. Giving all she had to her dear friend. Hoping there was still a chance.

River watched hopelessly. The sound of his temple pulsing was all he could hear. Swallowing hard he promises himself he wouldn't lose hope until all hope was gone. Riona had faith things would be alright. Maybe he needed more faith too.

"Leo," Kou whispers.

Taking her free hand Leo again forces a smile through the tears pooling in his eyes. "We did it. We can go home."

"You. You have to go without me."

"No." He shakes his head. "Nope," he revolves to sound positive. "You're going to be okay. We're going to be okay!"

"Take care of each other. Docter's orders."

Resting his forehead back onto hers Leo nods.

"I love-," Kou says in the breath that escaped her. Her hand she held over Riona now slipping.

River rests his ear on Riona's chest. Trying to hear a heart beat. Waiting. Waiting. Waiting. "I'm so sorry," River tells her in his mind.

Leo looks at Riv to meet his gaze. Their expression saying more than either one of them could ever say.

Reaching out River grips Leo's shoulder.

Chapter Fifteen

With the ground shaking and echoes of cheering that came steadily closer River knew who was coming. It was his father leading their tribe to battle on horse back. Now the barrier was down they came to assist further on taking back their land.

In the mean time Astra made her way up the hill to rejoin her worn fighters near the barrier. Approaching Leo and River she sees Kou and Riona laying side by side. Neither of them looked up to acknowledge her. They didn't have to.

Astra, herself, had bared much in her time. The many years took a toll on her. That was one thing different between herself and her sister. This war woke her sister up, much like it did Riona, but it wore her down. She was tired and couldn't wait for it to be over. When she became leader most of her emotions were shelved away. Much like now.

Not feeling the current situation properly she keeps to the task laid in front of them. That's what they were all fighting for. Kou and Riona knew such risks. "I know I don't have to tell you why they did this for us. I'm sorry for your loss, but this war is not over. I don't blame you if you think me insensitive, but let's not lose this war over the few we had to sacrifice. As hard as it may be. Leo. You know what we need to do now. Guide us through the next step. River, come with me, please."

Of course, Leo and River didn't want to leave, but there was truth was in Astra words. Leo bent down, kissing Kou's forehead. River finally letting go himself gives Riona's hand back to the grassy earth.

"Um," Leo starts. Wiping away any stray tears from his face before standing up. "We need to make sure to keep any remaining Rouge Droids off our backs while we find the main base of operations."

Astra leads the way and Leo follows. Through the barrier they walk. Not too far out sat a building. Without any Droids to protect them the Rouges would be next to powerless. To make sure of that River, Niigaanii, and all who came would stay near the barrier to keep any lingering Rouge Droids from going after Astra and Leo.

At one time in history the Rouges irrationally feared a future war with the physically gifted. That fear eventuality became reality by their own doing. Such fear held on for many generations without fail. It was time for all of that to end.

The Rouges focused all their attention on keeping the barrier up that they had spent all the Droids they had. Prideful of their mental gifts they had no fear that their technology could fail. Now they were without their main source of protection. The Rouges had no combat skills and they never used physical strength to fight. Their only strength they relied on was their mental capabilities. To a fault.

Astra and Leo traveled the outer walls until they came upon a door. Stepping in front, Leo begins picking the lock pad with the energy that came from his hands.

What he thought would be daunting task was unusually easy. Had he adapted to their technique? No. It was something else. He could feel it. Now that the barrier was down everyone had full access to their suppressed gifts! Leo could feel himself growing stronger every passing second.

Swish. The door opens.

Astra slips in first with Leo on her heel. They found themselves in a dusk lit setting. Traveling up the the hall they came to double doors with half windows. Ducking below the windows they came up to steal a peek occasionally.

The entire room was filled with Rouges sitting at their desks. They were unmoved. If they knew they were there they did nothing about it. It was plausible they were putting forth every effort to reestablish the barrier.

"How long would it take you to unlock these doors?" Astra looks up at him in anticipation.

"Not long. You probably already know your gifts are much stronger now the barrier is down. If all goes according to plan, once these doors open, I could theoretically shut down their power source. As long as..."

"As long what?" Astra cuts him off.

"The Rouges are extremely smart. They will do everything to keep me out. They may have back ups of back ups and cryptic passwords of passwords. Maybe. They likely never thought we'd get this far."

"They're smart, I got it. Outsmart them," Astra orders him.

Leo could feel the massive power coming from the whole building. He unlocked the door with ease without the Rouges noticing. Leo stops what he's doing. Perhaps he didn't need to see the system visually. It would take time to shut things down one at a time. All that was needed was to do is create a big enough power surge to crash everything. "I think I can take everything out. If I do that nothing may come back on again."

"Do it!"

Leo never created that big of a disruption before. The idea was logical, but was he strong enough to actually do it? Even with the barrier down there was no telling what was possible, but he had try. With a solar blue glow igniting on Leo's hands it crept up his arms before spreading to the rest of his body.

Checking to see if they were noticed by the Rouges Astra saw them working on some kind of code. Numbers and letters were running across the blackened part of their helmets. Sitting back down she was curious if they really didn't know they were there or if they didn't see them as a threat.

Quicker than a solar flare light from Leo's body extended from him. With all sounds of cracks and pops any electrical source was shattered. All went black.

"Great job," Astra complimented Leo, who was still glowing.

"Thanks."

"Now that we don't have to worry about the barrier going back up, let's figure out how to do more damage! You don't think you can keep this glow," she waves her hand over him, "on?"

Leo tilts his head not understanding her meaning.

"I have glow sticks." Astra lowers her head to search for them before she couldn't see.

Heading cautiously to the next hall they pause a moment before peeking around the corner. It was hard to see a arms length a way, but it seemed like they were in the clear. No signs of any Rouges or Rouge Droids. Light on their feet and glow sticks in hand they quickly made their way down the hall.

Turning the next corner Astra observed line like shadows dancing the floor. Could it be? Astra thought. "Is in anyone is here?" Astra calls out. "I'm with the alliance."

While they waited for a response they moved into position in case they needed to defend themselves.

"Astra? A uncertain voice comes from the darkness. "Astra, is that you?"

"Avyanna?" Astra waves Leo to follow her.

Rushing toward the bars their outstretched hands moved though them. "We had no idea if we would ever see you again," Astra told her sister.

"How's Riona?"

Astra's eyes slid away. "You would be so proud of her," Astra said her under her breath.

"Where is she?"

Astra couldn't bring herself to say it. That's when she heard footsteps from behind her.

"Riona was one of my best friends," Leo spoke slowly. "We're only here now because what she did. Our future is possible because of her."

Avyanna turns back to look at Astra who had tears welling in her eyes.

"I'm so sorry!" Astra cries out. "I'm so sorry I let you down."

Despite the truth of it Avyanna consoled her sister through the bars that separated them. Avyanna knew her sister well. She never showed her true emotions like this. She hadn't for a long time. It told her how much Riona changed her and she couldn't wait to hear more. "Please tell me all about her when we get out of here," she said with her cheeks wet.

That was another task. How would they get out? Once again Leo was already on the job. Unfortunately the cell, out of all things, was not digitally locked. But Leo finds the keys on the hanging wall! He tinkers with multiple keys trying to find the right fit. Click!

"We had no idea if they would execute," Astra voice trails off.

Avyanna spoke, "they very well could have, but my guess is they had something to prove to us. To show how much more evolved and superior they are. I know this may be an unpopular opinion but I think we should give them a choice when the time comes."

Leo holds his hand to Valdemar. "It's good to have you back, Sir."

"Leo was the one to break through the Rouges technology and bring it down," Astra told them.

"We will all be forever be grateful to you and all who contributed in making this happen," Valdemar tells him.

"You're very kind." Leo bowed his head in respect.

After a moment a silence Astra turns toward all there. "Let's get out of here!"

River, Niigaanii's alliance, the guardians, and many others came to barrier line when they saw Astra leading a group to them. They soon realized the previous leaders of Astra's alliance followed closely behind her.

Being all together each of the leaders of the alliances acknowledged them another with a nod or hand shake. Then all at once everyone there turned and bowed their heads respectfully to Valdemar and Avyanna. They endured more than most leaders. They wanted to show them their highest respect of having them back from capture and their express their sorrow for the loss of their daughter.

"We appreciate such expression," Valdemar spoke," but perhaps our old ways are just that. Everyone contributed something to this war. It was each and every one of you who made this possible. I'm not sure we should regain our position of royal leadership among the alliances. It seems you've all flourished fine without it. I motion we continue as it is right now, without it, and create something new for our new world."

Niigaanii steps forward. "Your majesty. Our world may have fallen back to us, but we still need wise leaders to guide us back in to the ways of our ancestors. I think I speak for all here when I say we have never had such good leaders among us as you, your wife, and your daughter. Continue the royal leadership line."

With all eyes on them Valdemar looks at Avyanna who nods. "Perhaps your right," Valdemar finally agrees.

"Then your leadership we will follow once again." Niigaanii holds out his hand.

While this conversation was taking place River was standing close enough to hear, but his thoughts pulled at him. He saw Riona's face clearly in his mind. Every feeling he had told him to go see her, but he fought against it. Yet, as if his body had a mind of his own he begins stepping forward before realizing it. No longer fighting he lets his feet guide him back to where Riona laid.

Stopping, he breaths in deep. Questioning if he really wanted to do this. It should have been him, he thought. Not the Riona and Kou. It should have been him.

When a strange twinge in his stomachs gnaws at him further he realized he had sensed something! That's what called him back. There was something that he was meant to find. Breathing in once more he steps closer.

Moving his eyes from Kou to Riona's body he stood there watching. With his eyes narrow and head tilted his eyes slide back to Kou. Her diaphragm raised slightly.

Dropping to Kou's side he had to make sure he wasn't seeing things. With his hand over her mouth he felt breath. Kou was breathing! "How is this possible?" he mumbles to himself.

He eventually concluded with the time the barrier had been down she somehow continued to heal herself with full assess to her gifts. Which made sense because he had felt her life! He never sensed something like that so strongly. What other explanation could be given?

Yelling over his shoulder others soon came to his side in disbelief. Of course, the last thing he wanted was for Riona's parents to see their daughter like this but it couldn't be helped. Helping Kou was what mattered right now.

Letting Leo take his place River approaches Riona's parents who had stopped shy of seeing their daughter. "Your majesty," he whispers. On catching Valdemar's gaze Rivers grief stricken eyes were unmistakable. Along with the gilt he felt in his heart. It was too much to bare. He would never be able to express how deeply sorry he was.

Those watching Kou gasped behind him. She was awake!

"Kou!" Leo squeaks.

"Leo." Kou's eyes flutter.

Peering down Kou lifts her shirt slightly to expose her wound. It was healing! The area was transitioning from a pink to a flesh toned color before their eyes. Not a scar remained. "I don't know how but I'm okay." Kou smiles in relief.

Leo was there ready to lift her to her feet when she turned to see Riona. Pushing him away her face sank. Crawling on her hands and knees to her friend she looks her over.

Whispers ran through the crowd of people watching her, but no one stopped her. Riona may be too far gone to be saved, but Kou would never forgive herself if she didn't try one last time.

Sitting next her Kou hovered her hands above Riona. Stopping briefly to realize how strong her gifts were. They were far more powerful than she remembered. Due to the heightened abilities she knew how her friend died and for how long. She still had time to repair some the damage, but even with full access to her gifts she didn't know if it would be enough to bring Riona back. Riona was past the point of a revival time frame.

Resting her hands over the wounds would Kou simply gave. In her own recovering strength, in her sadness, grief, love, and hope. She gave it all, but felt no life. Not wanting to give up tears travel down her face. Wishing she didn't have to let go. That's when she then felt a presence at her side, bracing her as she laid back. Those hands slowly guided her up to her feet. Away from Riona's unresponsive body.

Many were still there watching. The air became still and quiet aside from the trees that rattled their leaves softly. It was just enough to cover the sound of anxious heartbeats.

Standing close to his father River turns his face upward. A voice came into his mind. A voice he knew well. His thought's were already lonely without hers there. He had never known any Visionary to share thoughts as they had done. He knew the voice was a passing memory, yet it seemed so clear, like an echo from the past. That alone would be enough to torture him for all time.

Turning away from his father he fights the urge to see her again, so he walks away. When he was downhill and out of sight from the crowds he ran. Right into the closest tree. Falling into the grass he places his hands over his face. Trying to push all thoughts, sounds, and lingering memory of Riona out of his mind. It was too painful right now. Hands falling to his side he tries to focus. A breath in and a breath out to let it all go. He closes his eyes.

"River."

His eyes open. This wasn't a memory! He had heard her! He turned around and headed back in a haste. Despite being watched he knelt by her side. He observed the slightest of movement of her chest rising. It was so minimal anyone could have missed it. What Kou did must have worked!

"River."

"Riona! Kou! Kou, I can hear her."

Kou checked to confirm what River knew was true. Within in her chest Riona's heart came back to life. It took some time for her body to respond to Kou's aid but it did. Riona's body was repairing itself. "Riona! Riona can you hear me?"

River let Kou know Riona could hear her.

"Riona. Try to wake up for me," Kou guided.

While they were trying to help her wake her parents began calling her name. "Riona, baby, it's mom! Wake up for us. Riona, it's time to get up!"

River started shaking his head. "She's aware of everything but she can't wake up."

Kou places her hands on her face. "Whatever is happening is mimicking a coma, but I don't have a reason as to why. There's nothing I can do."

"What does that mean?" asks Valdemar.

"It means," Kou explains, "that she going to have to figure out how to wake herself, your majesty."

"Hey," River whippers in her ear. "Don't stop fighting, okay?"

"Did Kou call my dad, 'your majesty?'"

"There may be a few things I have yet to tell you."

"Oh, River. Okay, tell me."

"Each alliance has a chosen a leader. That you know. At one time the majority of our alliances were Visionary. The Visionary have had a long tradition among their people to have a head leader. A King or Queen if you may. Eventually that title would be passed to the most capable heir, if there was one. Currently, that royal blood line of leadership is your family."

"That why you call me Princess! I can't believe you hid that from me. River I-."

"What is it?"

"Your high hide."

"What?"

"Remember what I told you on your high hide!"

River scans his memories of that night. That was the night she kissed him. But, what did she tell him? He recalled the conversation of her thinking he was more gifted than he thought. How he realized he could manipulate emotions and share them. Was he missing something?

"River," Riona broke his thoughts. "How different would it be if you connected with me like that again and told me to wake up?"

"Could that really work?"

"There's only one way to find out."

Slipping his hand under her neck he places his forehead against hers and begins steadying his breathing. Slower and slower until it matched her sleeping sate. Closing is eyes he reaches out to her mentally. On doing so his consciousnesses was transferred into her sleeping mind.

With their connection he could feel her presence everywhere but she was nowhere to be seen. He walks forward through the dark void toward a dot of light, until he reached a flickering candle. Approaching, it came with sounds of whispering. Looking closer at the burning wick images start dancing in the flame. As the images grew larger, he was transferred to another place.

As he walked on, watching the images like a movie, he realized these were Riona's memories! It was her life! Her childhood, her time at the alliance, her hopes, and dreams. She was always a wonder, but her mind was even more so. Turning around he caught himself among her memories. Did he really look that way to her?

On looking straight River found himself, once again, in another a room. He didn't recognize it. Turning around he spotted a picture frame sitting on the dresser. Picking it up he saw Riona with her family. She was much younger but it was the still the same Riona he knew. It made him smile.

Picture in hand he turns to see a bed and in that bed Riona slept. It was her bedroom! No wonder why her mind took him here. This was her safe place.

Sitting on the side of her bed, next to her, he positions himself. With one arm wrapping around her shoulders and the other holding her hand he whispers in her ear to, "wake up." On doing so River lifted them both upwards.

Their connection broke and River found himself doing the same movement in the real word. Not a moment later Riona gasped for air and her eyes opened. Immediately looking up they fell into a hug.

"River."

"Hi princess."

Nigaannii was cheering and whooping, Riona's parents were laughing and crying all together, and Astra couldn't help but smile with them. Wiping a tear or two from her eyes.

River steadies Riona to her feet and within an instant she was squished by her parents. Soon thereafter her friends, Leo and Kou, both hugged her as well.

"So," Leo cuts in. "now that we accomplished what we set out to do," he looks at Valdemar and Avyanna, "what do we do now?"

"I think," Valdemar looks at his wife before looking at Riona. "I think it's time for Riona to take the lead on this one. What do we do Riona?"

Riona looked up at River with a grin curving up on her face. "I think I know."

She telepathically shared her thoughts with River and before long Riona and River intertwined their hands together. It was evident they were using and combining their gifts together. A rush of air was felt by all.

"What did you do?" Avyanna asks her daughter.

"We sent out a message to all that are willing to listen. Within time they will find us."

Three months later:

Riona walked among the tents. Their camp wasn't far from the barrier they took down three months ago. Since everything had been peaceful they decided to rebuild a life for themselves near the mountains. Homes were being built to accommodate any and all who needed or wanted them. This would be the start of their new society.

In those three months volunteers scouted to find more Rouge hideouts. Per request of Riona all Rouges were given a choice to join them. A handful of Rouges from each section did and a few helped them in their planning process. But the majority of the Rouges were locked and confined in their own buildings and they would remain there until they came to their senses. If ever.

Day after day Riona continued to wait for others who may have heard their message to come find them. A few, who had newly awoken their gifts, did seek them out. She knew it was only a matter of time when more would arrive.

Riona watched over borderline as she did every evening. Waiting for that time to come. Waiting for the rest of the world to realize who they once were. With the sun setting over the hills she turns to head back, but not before smiling. They did it. They really did it.

Walking past her best friends Kou and Leo she watched them playing with a few of the children who had arrived. Riona had never seen or heard so much happiness before. Riona promised herself that she would always be grateful for all she had and who she had in her life. Not all stories had a happy endings, but this was no ordinary story.

Up ahead River jogged toward her.

"Hey!"

"Hi." Riona smiles at him.

"We have company," he tells her.

Approaching closer they could see a man in a suit. It was the President! He was accompanied by only a few guards. Perhaps it was a private mission of curiosity?

Riona pushed a button on her watch and spoke, "Leo. I think you and Kou need to come see this."

Without delay Leo and Kou came to their side. Watching down the hills to see as well. Of all people to find them they were in awe that it would be President himself. The big questioned remained. What gift did he have?

The President singled out Leo and Kou immediately. Looking between the young adults staring back at him he asks, "who are you people?"

Riona steps forward, but on doing so she could see in the distance many more people heading their way. This was it. It was happening!

She rose her head high. "Welcome. We've been waiting for you. We promise to explain everything."

"Who are you?" the president asks again. His head tilting.

It wasn't very long ago Riona herself didn't know that answer. Now, she knew exactly who she was. Smiling she announces, "My name is Riona. Queen of the Visionary's."

Back of the book description:

Riona lives a sheltered life due to her parents dangerous occupation. Her parents planned to keep such occupation a secret until her eighteenth birthday, but before that could happen Riona's parents were taken from her. The truth about their life still unknown. Left to her own devices Riona takes matters into her own hands to find answers. Quickly learning that life wasn't what she thought it was she finds herself fighting for her parents cause.

Author: Melody Hope (Vanessa Guiney)
    Instagram: __melodyhope__
    Tiktok: melodyhope96
    Pateron: Melody Hope
    Email: horsedreamer3000@yahoo.com

Other books by Melody Hope
    Independent publishing and money making tips
    Secret of the Ocean *(Exclusively on Amazon)*
    My Nana's Purse *(Exclusively on Amazon)*
    Beyond the Music *(Exclusively on Amazon)*
    Mazy's Mystery and Mabel's Dance School *(Exclusively FREE on Smashwords)*
    Chasing Hearts *(Exclusively FREE on Smashwords)*

Coming soon
    Beyond the Music & Beyond the Lyrics *(A updated version of the previously published version of Beyond the Music along with its prequel)*
    A *(possible)* short film on the above series
    The Gifted *(A sequel to The Visionary)*

Don't miss out!

Visit the website below and you can sign up to receive emails whenever Melody Hope publishes a new book. There's no charge and no obligation.

https://books2read.com/r/B-A-LRQBB-QNTCF

BOOKS 2 READ

Connecting independent readers to independent writers.